SISTERS

©2018

Tanisha N Bowman

Sisters

DEDICATION

My beautiful daughter.

How blessed am I to have you? It's a question I've asked myself time after time, day after day, year after year. From the beginning, you have been my light, my motivation, and the best gift I've ever received. I thank the Higher Power every day for blessing me with you. Thank you for your encouragement and your unconditional love. I'd be lost without it and without you.

I love you Lai.

Photograph Courtesy of DeMayne Earvin Photography

Special Thanks

Paul Johnson III: Thank you for your beautiful poem. Your original piece added something to this story I never could. When I asked you to write something, I was unsure what I would get, but I knew it would be amazing. And I was not disappointed.

Touch of Class, SweetsByShiffawn, and All You Can Sweet, thank you for allowing me to use your businesses in this story. #BlackGirlMagic is real!!!

India. Arie, Jhene Aiko, Ledisi, H.E.R. and Ella Mai: Ladies, to honor your talent and beautiful music, if I could have built a soundtrack for this book, your names would be all over it.

To the readers whom have supported me from the Breeze Series, through Transitional Woman, and now to Sister: You are why I write. You are why I put my everything into these pages. Even if I only move one of you with my words, the late nights and long days were worth it. I hope you enjoy this story as much as I enjoyed writing it.

Prologue

A "Sister" is not always defined by blood. The trust, compassion, and respect you have for the woman sitting across from you makes you sisters. Fighting in a foxhole behind a firing line, with a woman watching your six and you watching hers makes you sisters. Phone calls at 2am from your ride or die when shit hits the fan and you gotta get outta your bed to get it right or console her heart, makes her your sister. Sitting in the dark with her listening to music that speaks of your heartbreak and loss makes you her sister. Happy hour drinks, birthday celebrations, and sista vacays makes you her sister.

We are built to protect to each other. That's the magic that makes us so beautiful and even threatening to some. Live in your magic Sis! Love your sister as much as you love yourself.

Let me introduce you to Lena, Kamryn, Miracle, and Zyera.

Lena

"Hi, I'm Lena. My full name is Dalene McCray but of course, as we do in black families, it's broken down to Lena. I love to be in my own space and can be in a room without being noticed unless I want to be. That's a talent I've had my entire life. Even as a child, I would find a quiet place and sit there out of sight. I can remember times when grown-ups forgot I was there and had conversations totally inappropriate for the ears of a child. I would listen all the same and would only be discovered once I laughed at something that was said. Then my mama would swat me on the butt and send me to where all the other children were located. This didn't change my actions though. Even in the presence of the other kids, I would go sit in a corner somewhere off to myself and dream about the life I would have when I was grown. Peace and solitude are all I wanted. When you come from a big family, that's all you ever really want when it's all said and done. Quiet. Silence."

"About me? I'm number three of five, with the breakdown of two girls and three boys. So that makes me the middle child. Overall, I'm not too hard to figure out. I try to live a simple life. Don't get me wrong, I like nice things and all, but I don't base my life on it. Being materialistic has never been my niche, however, I do like nice things. I mean, I drive a 2018 Mercedes coupe and own a three-bedroom, four-bathroom condo in one of the most upscale condominium communities in town. But be honest, who wants to drive a hooptie and live in the hood when they make six figures? Right, nobody! I live according to my means and spoil myself from time to time. I don't have any children, mostly because I never wanted the responsibility and partly because I didn't want to mess them up. I'm a great Auntie though! Lol. Probably the best on the planet. My nieces and nephews know that I'll do anything for them (within reason). I've paid for a few college educations, three sweet 16 cars, Disney Orlando trips, and a family cruise to the Bahamas. Hell, I've even let a few of them stay with me in my condo when one of my brothers or sister got into it with them. That's what aunts are for, right?"

"So now to the nitty-gritty, right? What man is my life? I spend time with a few fellas but there is one that I find myself completely drawn to and that's Michael. He's handsome, driven, sexy, and an entrepreneur. He owns Horns Lounge downtown and a small chain of coffee shops by the name of Café Cream, one of which is in the Concorde Building on the first floor, the same building where my office is. I met him in the building one morning as I was getting on the elevator. Somedays I feel like there's never enough hours in the day when I'm with him. He makes me laugh like no one else ever has. He makes me think about things I've never thought about before and the impact each thing alters my perspective a little bit, but in a good way. If I were smarter, I'd lock him down, but that's not my focus right now. I'm concentrating on building my legacy and my name."

Kamryn

"I'm Kamryn Slade. Who is Kamryn? A young and misunderstood, 21-year-old young woman, just starting out on her own. I'm single, no kids, no boyfriend, no girlfriend, but I do have a fish that is probably wondering why I haven't fed him in a few days. I'm an only child, which means I'm used to being. I come from a single parent home but I was raised in a lot of love. I never felt like I missed out on anything. My mom is EVERYTHING. When she was in her last few years of nursing school, she got pregnant with me. Instead of giving up and dropping out, she made the harder decision and kept me. She worked her ass off in school and made sure I had what I needed too. I never met my father. But I wasn't hurting for a positive male role model in my life. My grandfather stepped in and was there for me. He was and has always been my hero. Now, she's the Charge Nurse in the ICU at St. Lucian's Medical Center."

"Her goals for me have always been greater. What I wanted wasn't brought to the table for discussion. Until the day I sat down and told her my plans. Shocked doesn't cover the look on her face. She wasn't happy that's for sure. I was dropping out of college and moving to the city. Singing is my passion and to be a real singer, I needed to be where I could be discovered. Showing her support, she helped me get my first studio apartment above the pet store at Fifth and Chaser. She's friends with the couple who owns the building and they told my mom they would look after me, of course, that helped too. She paid my rent for the first six months to give me time to get settled and in true Mom fashion, she bought me a bed, tv, small sofa, and some food for my refrigerator and cabinets. Before leaving she slid $300 in my back pocket when we hugged. After she left, I found an envelope on my bed with $500 and a note saying, "Just in case the $300 isn't enough." I laughed and texted her thank you with the heart emoji. Moms, huh, you gotta love them."

"I was in the city for three weeks when I saw the "Help Wanted" sign in the window at Horns and went in to apply. The owner hired me on the spot for the waitress spot. After a few months, I moved to bartending. Then one night, after closing, I found the courage to sing for the owner. I'm guessing I blew his mind, cuz he agreed to let me sing with the house band Thursday, Friday, and Saturday nights. And told me I could keep bartending Monday, Tuesday, and Wednesday. I'm not banking but I'm still able to save some of it to pay for studio time. In my mind, I'm going to be the big star, selling out stadiums and arenas with ticket prices for a grand for the front row. Singing and dancing and smiling the whole time. Hearing crowds scream my name and cry over me when I hit the stage. That is the life I want to live. I want to go on a world tour with opening acts and backstage interviews. Have screaming fans who beat down my security trying to get to me. Yeah, that's the life I want to live."

"Unfortunately, I'm not dating right now. I have more important things on my plate."

Miracle

Time for my introduction. "Good afternoon, I'm Miracle Griffins. My parents named me Miracle because they told me that's what I was for them, their miracle child. My parents were both older when they had me. They had been married 30 years before I came along and I was their only child. Having given up hope for a child they built a life with each other. And then out of the blue, here I come. They were so happy to finally have a child, they gave me everything I ever wanted or could dream of. They loved me beyond rhyme or reason. I would have to say they were the best parents anyone could ever have. I couldn't imagine a better Mom and Dad."

"I remember my friends asking me if having older parents was a drag. I would tell them it was the best. They had lived so much of their lives without children they were ready for me and anything I could think of doing to get over on them. My mama gave the best advice on everything and my Daddy was so loving and protective. Any man that meets me has big shoes to fill if he ever hopes that I will love him the way I loved my Daddy. I guess that's what caused me to be so hard on men."

"One night, while driving home from one of my dance recitals, some asshole ran a red light and ran into the side of our car. My mother was killed on impact and my father lived on a ventilator for three days. I was eleven years old and walked away with just some bruising and couple scratches from the broken window glass. I still remember their double funeral with matching shiny black caskets. After the funeral services, I went home with my Grandma and sat in my room. It had been decided that since my parents' house (which was now mine) was paid for, my Grandma would move in so that I could stay in my same school with my friends. I was told later, the decision was made because I had already lost so much, they didn't want me to lose anything else."

"My parents were very responsible with their lives and with mine. To make sure I would be taken care of in the event they passed, they had very generous life insurance policies on themselves, naming me as their sole beneficiary. In all, it totaled one million dollars. There were stipulations to the money. One was a clause referencing college and the remaining was set up in a trust for me, to be released to me sporadically when I was 16, 18, and 21. My grandmother never touched a penny and she wouldn't let anyone come in and touch it either. She took care of me with her retirement and the social security checks she received as my guardian. Even with the loss of my parents, I didn't find the need to search for love, my Grams gave me all the love I could ever want or need."

"I'm a college graduate, however, I have no ambition to find a job, but with half a million dollars left from my parents' life insurance do I really need a job right now? I can live off half a mill for at least five years if I'm mindful of how I spend my money. I still live in my childhood home alone. Even after doing some renovating and redecorating, I still feel the presence of my parents when I walk in the front door. It brings me peace just being there. Many have told me, I'm lucky because of the money. But I'd trade every penny of it to have them   walk   through   those   doors   again."

Zyera

"Good evening. My name is Zyera Danes. I don't think my age is important as I'm sure it carries no true value. I'm a wife, a mother of three grown men, and a grandmother of two, one girl and one boy. My husband is the world-renowned Eric Danes. That's right, standing 6 feet 4 inches tall, with green-eyes and blonde hair, he is the most sought-after plastic surgeon to Hollywood's elite. He's fixed more butts, breasts, noses, and jawlines than the Department of Transportation fixes roads. Hard to believe he's married to a black woman huh? But he is. All this natural booty and beauty has been with him since he was in medical school. My sons have all grown into their own men who are successful in their own rights. I am proud of each of them for following their own hearts and goals. My oldest, Eric Jr., his wife Evelyn, and my two grandchildren live in Georgia. They're both attorneys. My middle son, Edward, owns several small businesses in town. And my youngest son, Evan, owns a health and wellness company with a team of trainers, nutritionists, and health specialists. I'm still trying to figure out why the last two decided to stay here instead of branching out to other locations. But they are my babies and I'll always support them."

"Me? I'm just your average well-kept woman. I don't want for anything but I have everything I could have ever dreamed about. I am always presentable and never have a hair out of place. I host dinner parties and events on my estate with my husband and dine with the mayor at least once a month. I am what most women are striving to become. I did what women do. I supported and helped my husband build his business, our business, to be what it is today. It was my Masters in Business Administration, Marketing, and Accounting that made my husband's practice so lucrative. It was my long nights, in the beginning, writing business plans and networking that made him the man he is today. This is not "Waiting to Exhale" and I'm not about to be like Bernie, emptying out the closet and setting his shit on fire in the driveway. Naw baby! That man knows who made and built him. I made sure my name is on everything that he owns right alongside his. Co-owners, partners, and all that good shit. That man didn't come from money. We built this empire together. No prenuptial agreement here. My mama didn't raise no damn fool. To be completely honest, I own 52% of the business and as majority shareholder, I can make any decision I wish and no one can stop me. But, I don't get myself involved in the operation as much as I used to. It doesn't interest me in that way. My husband continues to do what he's doing to secure the bag."

"I'm from a small country town in South Carolina. I knew from an early age I was going to get out of there as soon as I could and that's exactly what I did. The day after I graduated high school, I got on a bus and headed north. I had one hundred and fifty dollars in my bra, my one little brown suitcase, and a dream. I was accepted into a small community college then transferred to a major university. I made a way for me to be successful to be able to live the life I wanted."

Chapter One

Friday night at Horns, with live music and a caramel skinned woman singing along with the house band. A soulful voice floats over the crowd as she sings her own rendition of Ledisi's "Forgiveness." The passion in her voice makes us all believe she's singing directly to someone who none of us can see. "You owe me my forgiveness." She sings as the chorus starts. Her head dips back and she takes a deep breath to belt out a vocal run that no one expects to hear. The crowd that has been quietly listening now erupts in a combination of applause and whistles at her talent and even more at her level of comfort on stage. Kamryn Slade's naturally curly auburn hair glows like a halo from the stage lighting. The stage fan in the left wing slowly blew her curls away from her face as her beautiful voice continued to hypnotize the full house of patrons who came just for her. Friday night was a busy night for Horns, especially since the owner signed Kamryn to sing with the band three nights a week.

It is all she dreams it to be. In her heart, Kamryn knows this is where she belongs. On stage, not just singing but entertaining a crowd of people with their eyes fixed on her and only her. Waiting to hear what note she will sing next and make each lyric her own. Waiting to close their eyes and feel each word as if she is singing directly to them or for them. Her love and her passion float over them as they watch in awe. It's magic, live and in person. The faces of each person solidify her thoughts and make her dig deeper to give them exactly what they have come here to receive. All of Kamryn, every inch of her spirit and her soul as she creates vocal runs on the fly and the band accommodates when she runs over the beat. They pause when she hits a point and is acapella. The room holds its breath all at once to hear the purity of her untrained and perfect pitch. No waver, no shake, no fear, and no hesitation. Just her sound. The bartender stops making drinks and all conversation has ceased. No sidebars here. All faces fixed towards the stage and all eyes and ears tuned in to Kamryn.

"If the blind lead the blind, which one is wrong? I blame myself for letting you make me stoop so low. Hate me now but you taught me everything." I sing, like the song was written just for me.

"Yes ma'am!" Someone says from the audience. That is all Kamryn needs to hear and allows her voice to fly free. She opens her mouth and lets the most amazing vocal run fill the air. And then there's quiet. The entire room stands on their feet for her first ever standing ovation. The band goes back into the song and Kamryn finishes the song to a standing room only crowd.

"Thank you. Thank you. Wow, I am floored."

"No baby," a man says. "We are amazed by you." The rest of the room agree with whistles and cheers.

"You are all too kind. Thank you so much. Please enjoy the band as they soothe your souls with their smooth sounds. I'll be back." I step off the stage to walk over to the bar for a drink. Several patrons stop me to shake hands and tell me how much they enjoyed my last song. I smiles and say "thank you" as I move through the sea of table and chairs. It's crowded tonight and it feels so good. At the bar I sit in a barstool on the corner. The bartenders for the night are CT and Banks and they are my favorites. They have turned into my big brothers in a city where I didn't grow up and have no real ties. Having people, you can truly trust is essential and after time they become family.

"You are killing em tonight Kam." CT says. "Where did that run come from girl? You had us over here high fivin and shit."

"I don't know, I just felt it and let it go."

"Well damn! That shit just shut this whole place down. Ain't no way they gone let you go anywhere else and sing now. Everybody in this place tonight said they were here because they heard your voice was better than the Queen B herself." He hands me a bottle of water, leans over the bar, and kisses my cheek. "If you keep packing this place, you may want to start asking for a cut from the cover charge. Michael raised the cover to $20 a few weeks ago and added a three-drink minimum. There are at least one hundred and fifty people in here on a Thursday night and there's still a line outside. He's making money hand over fist and what is he paying you? Banks and I are making better tips than usual. It's because you are mesmerizing them with those vocals."

"I did get a small raise a few weeks ago but you know it's not about the money for me CT. It's about being up on that stage and doing what I love. Watching the faces of the people listening to me as I give my heart to them in the words of every song. When I'm up there, I feel like I'm on a huge stage during my own concert. I feel amazing and free!"

"Well, at least you're getting a little more money, Sis. Tomorrow we are sure to be packed after seeing what tonight is like. Word travels fast and with your voice, I'll bet it's moving like lightning through other clubs. You make sure whatever you have set to sing is on point. There are a lot of people in town this weekend from NYC, LA, and even Chicago. With the way you're packing this place, I'm sure a few of them may make their way in there to listen to live music. Be ready Sis. Be ready. We all love you here and we want what's best for you for real. We ain't on some bullshit trying to pump you up for a big fall. We see your talent even more than you do. Be ready, you hear me? Anything can happen around here at any time. Always be on your game baby girl. Always."

The look on his face is clear and I know he's being as truthful and honest as he has ever been with me. "I hear you and I will be."

He smiles at me again, then gets himself back to work pouring drinks as the customer orders. I sip my water as I waits for the band to finish their "intermission" musical selections. This is the time I've been using to people watch. Tonight's crowd is so lively and everyone is having a wonderful time. There is laughter coming from a table on my left which draws my attention. At this moment, I can't imagine it getting any better than this for me. I scan the room once more and stop at a table closer to the door, where a woman sits alone.

"Am I crazy or is that lady staring at me?" I ask myself out loud. "No, she can't be." I look for CT to get his attention but he's busy charming some woman out of her phone number to notice me. My eyes look back to the table to get a better look but the woman is gone. "That was weird."

The band brings their song to an end and I walk through the sea of tables and chairs again to retake my place up on the stage. "Let's give Soulful Sounds another round of applause. I love singing with them. People have asked me, why do I let a live band play for me when I sing? But I make sure to correct them and tell them, it's the band who allows me to sing with them. And I wouldn't have it any other way. I am so grateful to them for letting me sit in with them to share my voice with them and with you all. I am just as appreciative of you for coming out tonight and showing me so much love." The crowd whistles and claps as the members of Soulful Sounds take bows.

"Before the break, I sang "Forgiveness" by Ledisi, which is one of my most favorite songs. Now I want to share with you my rendition of a song close to my heart. This song and this artist has been a true inspiration to me as I chase my dream of being a singer. I've learned to be true to myself in all forms and fashion. This artist has always shown that she is true to herself and never compromises who she is for the industry or anyone else. From growing her sisterlocks to the big chop. She continuously and consistently is showing us that she is comfortable in her Brown Skin. India.Arie reflects the strength and courage to be just who she is. Her song, "Beautiful" from the Secret Life of Bees soundtrack, has been one of my favorites since I was a child. And I am honored to share my rendition of it with you tonight if you will let me."

"Yeah!" The crowd yells back at me.

"Thank you." The band begins to play. "The time is right, I'm gonna pack my bags. And take that journey down the road." I sing. Immediately, I feel the song take over me, transforming me. I step off the stage and walk through the crowd. The spotlight follows me as I weave in and out of the sea of table. Everyone is watching and each person I come close to smiles. Some are mouthing the words and sing along with me. "I wanna go to beautiful, beautiful, beautiful."

The crowd again falls under my spell, as they sway to the beat of the music, the melody-mix of the guitar strings and my voice. This is where I'm supposed to be. This is home. This is right.

Chapter Two

It's leg day, I hear inside my own head as I walks into the gym. I see my trainer waiting for me by the free weights and bench press impatiently. Getting my mind ready for what my body is about to go through always takes self-motivation. Multiple sets of squats, deadlifts, leg press, thigh press, and the glute machine. Ugh, I hate leg day but loves how my lower body has rounded out. Maleek waits with his whistle around his neck waiting for me so we can get this workout started. He looks down at his watch, then back at me with a frown on his face. The normal response to her lateness.

"Whenever you're ready princess. I'm on your time but don't think you're going to cheat me out of a full workout today." He lets that devilish smile cross his mouth showing his perfect teeth. I can feel my face get warm from imagining the other things his lips can do. Instead of dwelling on it, I close my eyes to concentrate on the tasks ahead.

"My bad Maleek, I got caught in traffic."

"Yeah, whatever Miracle. Save the excuses for all the breath you're going to need on this ass kickin I'm about to give you." He claps his hands together twice and motions for me to start stretching. "Alright, hands up high and reach. Bend at the waist and touch the floor. Hold at the bottom 9, 8, 7, 6, 5, 4, 3, 2, 1. Now spread your feet apart and repeat the stretch. Hold at the bottom 9, 8, 7, 6, 5, 4, 3, 2, 1. And repeat." They go through several more stretches to get her lower body muscles ready for the pain she knows he's about to unleash during his rigorous workout plan.

"Alright, let's hit these squats. Last week we worked on 65lbs, this week we're moving to 75lbs. In three sets of fifteen. You ready?"

"Yes." I position myself at the bar and begins my first set of lifts as Maleek watches in the mirror. He corrects my posture and positioning as he counts. My eyes move from watching my body and form to his look at his eyes in the mirror. From my perspective, I swear he's watching my ass. Maybe I'm wrong. I look at him again and follow the path of his eyes. Ummm, yeah, he's watching.

"Push your butt out more Miracle. Make your arch deeper. Seven, six, five, four, three, two, one. Ok, rest for thirty seconds."

Oh, never mind. Well damn. I reset the bar and step away.

"Job in place to keep moving, don't stand still. You want your muscles to keep working." He never looks up when he's talking, he's counting the seconds. "Alright get ready."

I repeat this exercise to finish the set and move on to the rest of my workout. Throughout the next hour and a half, I watch him more than I'm watching my own actions. Maleek catches me a few times but doesn't show any reaction. He keeps it professional and takes me through the routine of exercises. By the end of the session, I've worked up a decent sweat thanks to him. I check my watch to verify my time is up then prepare myself to say my good-bye.

"Hold up girl. I have something extra for you today. I knew you were going to be late, so I've reserved the octagon for us for 30 minutes. Let's go, I'm going to teach you something new today."

"Awe damn Maleek! Come on, I'm tired."

"Save that shit for someone who cares girl. Let's go." He walks out of the main gym and into the large workout room. It contains one boxing ring surrounded by four small octagons used for MMA training.

"I don't know anything about this kind of stuff. I don't want to get hurt. Why do I need to learn this? The workout we already do is good enough for me and I'm tired as hell after that workout you put me through."

"I know, that's why I wanted to teach you some things. Don't worry, I'm not charging you extra for it. I want to add some of this into your workout to switch it up every now and then, plus it will teach you some techniques on how to protect yourself."

"Why does that matter to you if I can protect myself?" Trying to be cute, I tilt my head.

"Listen. What happens to you matters to me. I'm not just your trainer, I'm your friend. Well, at least I hope you consider me a friend."

"A friend huh? Ok. Show me what you got."

We step into the octagon ring and he closes the fenced door. One the floor are two sets of gloves for both of us and a set of boxing pads to use. "Put on the gloves." He points to the smaller pair of gloves.

"I'm just going to show you a few self-defense techniques you can use on the spur of the moment if you need to. We'll go slow at first and then speed it up for a live go." He smiles to try and make me more comfortable. He puts his hands up. "Get your hands up. Keep the right closer to your face to protect it. Put your left foot forward." I must have been standing awkwardly because he drops his hands and walks over to me. Positioning his hands on my waist, he turns the angle of my torso to the right, drops to one knee and slightly moves my left foot forward. I can feel my skin flush from the touch of his hands on my waist. My skin gets so hot that it feels like he's burning his fingerprints into my waistline. My mind begins to wonder but the sound of his voice brings me back to reality. "This is what I meant. No one can hit you head on if you're standing is at an angle." He steps back tilts his head and puts his hands back up. "Ok, now let's go through some movements. I'll go slow, ok?"

"Ok."

He pauses before continuing. "Do you trust me?"

"Yes. I trust you." I admit as I looks deep into his eyes. It's at this point that I realize, my answers cover so much more than the limited meaning of his question.

He smiles, "Alright girl, let's try this out. Put your hands back up." He winks and I smile back, following his instructions to get back into my fighting stance. "You ready?" I nod to confirm and we begin. As promised, he proceeds slowly taking each movement slowly and in phases to show me the correct way to throw a punch, block a punch, and even counterpunch. We practice like this for about ten minutes and then he speeds up his movements.

"You're catching on quickly, that's good! Your movements are fluid already and your response to my aggression is fast. That is very good. Have you taken any martial arts classes before?"

"Thank you. No, I haven't. You're just a good teacher."

"Well, you know, I do what I can and work with what I got." He says and laughs. "Now I'm going to teach you a couple ways to take someone down and how to get away if you get taken down. You ready?"

Most of me wants to say no I'm not ready, partly because I don't want Maleek that close to me and I surely don't want him possibly on top of me. That might be too much right now, especially the way my hormones have gone from zero to one hundred in less than thirty seconds. Just the thought of it is making my heart race and my mind wander. "Ok, yes I'm ready."

"Alright, let's go." He steps closer and even after all the sweating they've done today, he still smells amazing. Stuck in my own head, I don't notice him grabbing me to knock me off balance. We both fall to the mat as he lands on top of me. My eyes close as I try not to look at him.

"Shit, are you ok? I didn't mean to fall on you so hard."

I open them to see true concern in his eyes as he scans my face. "I'm fine. You just caught me off guard. I'm fine." I close my eyes again.

"Then why are your eyes closed?" Again, there is worry in his voice.

"Because." It seems that is all I can convince my voice to say. I can't tell him the true reason why my eyes are closed and my breathing has become shallow. This man is giving me goosebumps and hot flashes. Part of me wants to push him off but the feeling of him on top of me has my mind second thinking that action.

He leans slightly to one side, still partially covering my body as he continues to watch my face. Again, I open my eyes and look directly into his. They soften with passion as he scans my face and raises his hand to touch my cheek. "Are you sure you're ok Miracle? The last thing I want to do is hurt you." He strokes my cheek softly. I shift my eyes to look slightly over his shoulder.

"Yes. I'm fine. You just caught me off guard, that's all."

"That's all huh? You sure about that?" He leans in closer. He opens his mouth and the smell of mints emerges on his breath. Our noses are almost touching and he smiles. "Correct me if I'm wrong, but there is something going

19

on here. You're not saying anything, but your body is reacting to me. I can feel your nipples getting harder under my chest. Your breathing has gotten faster. Your heartbeat has sped up and I can feel it beating through your chest. Your right hand hasn't left my bicep since we hit this mat and you won't keep your eyes open long enough for me to look at them. Tell me what's going on with you and why are you keeping your eyes closed?" He strokes my cheek once more.

This turn of events and change of air in this small space has me weak in the knees. If I were standing, the lightest feather would be able to knock me over with the slightest touch. My voice has all but disappeared as I try to express my feelings or better yet, try to hide them. But a sudden bout of shyness has me blushing from Maleek's obvious read of my body's reactions. Not even as a teenage girl did I react to boys in this manner when they showed me attention or interest. For some reason, this is different. I feel it deep within.

"Nothing is wrong. I lost my breath after the fall. For real. I'm fine." I tap his bicep that I've been holding on to since my back hit the mat.

"Girl, tell me the truth. I'm not letting you up until you do. And you know I'm strong enough to hold you here all day."

"You ask me questions you already know the answers to. Is that to torture me or to get me to say what you want to hear? Either way, that's a little narcissistic don't you think?"

"Call it what you want. But you are going to say it." He smiles and runs his hand from my cheek down to my neck and trace the outline of my body. He stops the trace at my hip and rests his hand there.

I raise my eyes to gaze into his and drop them again. "You have a way of affecting me like no other man ever has. You make me nervous and laugh at the same time. You make me feel safe and scared all at once. How is that even possible? You've been my trainer for almost a year now and you have taken my body through major changes. Not that I was out of shape before I started with you, but you have molded my body to be the lean and curvaceous piece of art that it is. I sometimes think you have molded it this way for you more than for me."

He smiles at my last statement and lets out a chuckle.

"I'm serious you know. I do think that you are creating this body for you. For you to touch, to tease, and to please. But that's just a dream right. A fantasy. You wouldn't be, couldn't be interested in me." My eyes meet his.

"Miracle, you are a beautiful young woman and any man would be lucky to have you in his life and on his arm. I guess I include myself in that statement. I've never mixed business with pleasure but you have me rethinking that way of operating too. I can't lie, girl, there's something about you and I can't put my finger on it. I enjoy our professional relationship but I have thought about more. And before you ask, no, this is not what this part of the training session was about. It's just after seeing how you have reacted to me today, I couldn't hold it in any longer."

"I'm a virgin." And time stops and everything around us appears to freeze from my words of confession. I feel my cheeks warm from embarrassment.

He tilts my chin so my eyes find his. "I know." His eyes drop to my lips then come back to my eyes. "Would you like to go out sometime?"

Chapter Three

"Good morning, what can I help you with this morning?"

"Good morning. I would like a tall white chocolate macchiato with an extra shot of espresso, whip cream, and three sugars."

"Absolutely ma'am. What name would you like for me to place your coffee under?"

"Lena." I say to her.

"Great, your total is $3.45."

I hand her my black card to pay for my coffee. From the corner of my eye, I notice a woman eyeing me from head to toe. I try to shake it off, thinking she must appreciate a well-dressed woman. With my transaction complete, I step away from the counter and place the card in my wallet then step aside to allow the next customer to place his order. Over my shoulder, I notice a woman watching me, but shake it off because I don't recognize her face. I look away, then back to her as she peers down at her phone. I check my watch for the time and notice it's 7:30 am, I have forty-five minutes before my first meeting. I look around the café to see if Michael is here somewhere.

"Looking for someone?" The sound and smoothness of his voice give me goosebumps every time. I smile but don't give him the satisfaction of turning around. I act as if I don't hear him to see what his next move will be. "Oh, so you gone stand here and act like you don't hear me?" He asks and steps closer to whisper directly in my ear. "I know you hear me, woman. You must want me to smack you on yo ass right in the middle of my place of business. I don't give a damn about this crowd. People always lookin for a show anyway. Waitin for a reason to whip out their cell phones and start recording at any and everything that happens these days. I can give them a show or you can pay me some attention. I mean, it's not like you slept in my bed last night. I called but you didn't answer your phone. Guess you were out with that other nigga. He ain't putting in work like me though? Wanna know how I know that? Cuz you never get coffee the next morning after being with me. I wake you up, pussy first, so

22

you don't need that caffeine. I'm your caffeine." He steps closer and eliminates the small space that was remaining. I feel his dick rub against my ass but still, I continue to face forward. "I'll give you five seconds to rectify this situation before I act like a street nigga up in here and show the fuck out. Five. Four. Three." He chuckles. "Woman you are trying my patience. Two."

"Tall white chocolate macchiato with an extra shot, whip cream, and three sugars for Lena." The young man whose name tag read "Anthony" says. Over my shoulder he looks at Michael and mouths, 'sorry Boss.'

"Right here." I raise my hand and step towards the counter to collect my coffee. "Thank you." I get to the door where Michael is still standing. He checks me up and down with his eyes and steps out to holding it open for me.

"You look even better from the front. Hmmm. I'll see you later Lena." He winks.

"Yes, you will." I kiss his cheek and proceed to the elevator for my ride up to the 26th floor. I step on the elevator and turn around making direct eye contact with Michael. He winks his eye again and smiles. I nod my head and wink back as the elevator doors close.

The ride up is quiet besides the instrumental jazz that plays over the intercom. We stop at the 10th, 11th, 21st, and 23rd floors before finally making it to the 26th. I step out and almost right into my assistant Cassandra. She smiles.

"You just saw Michael, didn't you?"

"How do you know that?"

"Lena, you always have that smile on your face after you run into him downstairs. I know that smile girl. What did he say? More importantly, what did he do?"

"Nothin new. Appeared out of nowhere like Harry Houdini and was all up on my ass. Tryin to get me excited in a café full of damn people." I laugh, remembering his words and his threat. I can admit, the threat was my favorite part. I wonder what he would have done if he got to one?

"What's that smile for? He must have said something more than what you're telling me. But you know what? It's cool, no worries. I won't try to beat it out of you. You'll tell me sooner or later." We enter my office and she goes right into work mode. "You're 8:15 am call with Mr. Sykes was pushed back to 8:30 am. Mr. Sykes' secretary called to say he was running a little late and asked if we could adjust the time. I checked your schedule first and made the change. After that, you have a 10 am with Mrs. Mauthers and Mr. Grande to talk about their newest contracts. Following that, is the Ladies of Pearl luncheon from noon until 2 pm at the Michelle Obama Essence Gallery. Finally, you have one last conference call at 3:00 pm to bring your day to a close. Do you have any questions?"

"I think I'm good. Are you coming to the luncheon with me?"

"Yes. I have your speech ready and we'll be sitting at the front table with the President and Vice President. And before you ask, I've already had a car and driver already reserved. The doorman will call up once the car arrives."

"Great. See that's why I hired you."

"You hired me because I'm your best friend. You keep me employed because I'm the best at what I do and I'm never going to let you down."

"True, true. Anything else going on I need to know about?"

"No, not that I can think of right now. I'll be in my office if you need me. I already emailed your new schedule to Ms. Peaches to let her know what's going on with you today. And remember you are out of the office tomorrow all day for the ribbon cutting ceremony at the hospital uptown."

"I remember." I sit at my desk as Cassandra uses the adjoining door between our offices to enter her own. After five minutes, Ms. Peaches rings my line to let me know Mr. Sykes is on the phone. "Thank you, Ms. Peaches, you can send him through." My phone rings and my day begins as planned.

Chapter Four

Today is going to be busy. As I drink my first glass of water for the day, I look at my planner and see the two most important events to attend. The Ladies of Pearl luncheon is this afternoon for our annual Exemplary Women in the Community event. As chairwoman of the committee, I'll be there to present the awards to our selected women and of course to make sure that everything goes as planned. The honorees this year are a fresh group of women who have made their marks on our community through partnerships and charity work. There were originally thirty women nominated this year. Several of them, I had not heard of before however, that is no surprise as they do not associate with my inner circle. After researching their efforts and accomplishments in the community, I was pleased to learn and read all the amazing things they brought to our city. Narrowing down the list to seven was a challenge for our voting committee as we wished we were able to honor them all. This year, we decided to change the program and give the ladies who did not make the top seven honorary mention. It felt like the appropriate thing to do, to show that our organization recognizes appreciates their achievements in our community. Before the luncheon, I have a doctor's appointment to have some blood drawn that ordered last week. Dr. Mahoning called me yesterday and asked me to stop by her office today.

"Good morning love." Eric kisses my cheek as he slides past me to get to the coffee pot. "How did you sleep?"

"Not bad honey. You, however, were out like a light and snoring like a grizzly bear." I laugh.

"I know. I had two long surgeries yesterday. One facelift and one breast alteration. Let me tell you, this life I live is so full of fun stuff. I even had an appointment yesterday with a new client. She came in to see me about having her nose done and she's only fifteen. I couldn't believe it, babe. A nose job at fifteen. She was very definite about it too. Child stars are sometimes the worst. The worst part about the whole thing is that there is absolutely nothing wrong with her nose." He shakes his head at the whole situation. "I can't imagine at fifteen wanting to alter anything on my body."

"That's because you are perfectly perfect my dear. There is nothing on your body that you need to alter. Even at this age, you are looking fine as ever."

"You're only saying that because of that big rock on your hand." He laughs again and comes to stand behind me, placing his arms around my waist. "You, my beautiful queen, are like a fine wine. Just getting better with time. How did I get so lucky to marry a woman like you?" He pulls me into him.

"With corny ass lines like that one. I like stuff like that." I say and we both laugh.

"Do you remember how the brothers in college used to stare at us? I know they were jealous because I had the sexiest woman on my arm all the time. I remember the death threats I would get under my dorm door when we first started going out. They hated me, I mean truly hated me because you chose me over any of them. Honestly, I couldn't believe it myself at first. I was so geeky with my glasses and pocket protector. And you were this beautiful goddess that I would watch from across the room in our English Literature course. The day I worked up the courage to come sit by you was the best day of my life. I remember the first thing you said to me."

"I do as well." I say and lean back into him.

"Are you lost or something white boy?" We say in unison and laugh together. He steps behind me as he kisses the back of my neck. I feel him get excited through his slacks.

"Why are you playing with me, love? You know I didn't get any of this good loving last night. Now you trying to hold out on me?" his voice is raspy with passion.

"You see how my body still reacts to you?" He tells me in between kisses. "I could eat you right now. Just lift you up and place you on this counter. I know you don't have any panties on underneath this robe, you never do." His hands slowly untie the sash and my robe falls open. Turning me around as he takes a step back to allow me just enough space to spin. I look into his blue eyes and see the hunger in them.

"Baby, you know Olivia is here by now and the rest of the staff will be here shortly. You can't put me on this counter and have your way. Someone will walk in on us and I'll be too embarrassed. At least take me upstairs where we can close the door. This is not the place."

"I can't wait. I want to taste that chocolate kiss that's peeking out of those perfect lips. Don't make me take you upstairs for that. This is my house and if eating my wife on this counter is what I want to do, then dammit that's exactly what I'm going to do. I paid for this marble countertop that you picked out and I'm having my breakfast right here. And don't worry about Olivia, I sent her to the store for some things. The rest of the house staff won't be here for another hour. Now that's enough talking. I didn't get to do this last night and you are the only thing I want for breakfast." His smile captivates me as his hands grasp my waist and lift me onto the countertop.

He parts my legs like Moses and steps his 6'4" frame between them never breaking the connection between his eyes and mine. Pulling my ass to the edge of the counter to allow him full access to what he wants, he lowers his body until what he wants is right in front of him. Finally, breaking eye contact, he kisses my most sensitive spot softly. My hand instinctively moves from his shoulder to the back of his head, gripping him between the nape and the neck. So close, I can feel his breath on me as he admires my cleanly waxed kitty.

"Hmm. Just the way I like it," he whispers then looks up at me. "Thank you." he exclaims as he squeezes my ass and buries his head in between my legs. I feel his cold tongue inside of my warm spot as he alternates between kissing and penetration.

"Oh Eric," is the only thing I can manage to say. This man knows my body like no other man ever has. He can bring me to orgasm in three minutes flat. But that three minutes always feels like hours from the ecstasy that comes with it. I swear it feels like he takes a piece of my soul every time.

"Yes, my love," is his response as he devours me on the kitchen counter. The sounds he makes seems to resonate from his toes. Deep moans as he slurps and sucks. His hands moving with the motions of my hips as I lean back on the counter and he places my legs on his shoulders.

You know how you can tell a man loves the taste of his woman? By the energy, he puts into pleasing her. By the way, he revels in the taste of her. His eagerness to get the scent of her on his tongue and suckle on the most sensitive part of her body with his lips. His mission is to make her physically and mentally shake from the pleasure he brings her knowing that no other man can do to her what he can. To know her body in a way that no one else ever will. Letting her know that he is hers and she is his. Not in an ownership sense, but a spiritual sense as their bodies become one. On cue, my body begins to shake and Eric snuggles in closer as he knows what is about to come down. Firming his grip on my hips to make sure I can't run, he does the thing that makes me explode. My hands grab onto his shoulders and my back arches pushing my shoulders into the counter.

"Oh, gawd." As one of my hands makes its way to my left breast.

"Yes!" Eric says never moving from where he is. "I'm ready baby. Give me what I've been waiting for."

I feel the fire from the top of my head move down through my body. My hips move counterclockwise as Eric's head move clockwise. The fire reaches my abdominal areas and prepares to cum as my husband grabs my thighs pushing them further apart. Shallow quick breaths escape me and I begin to shake uncontrollably.

"Yes, baby. Cum for me."

And on command, my body releases for him as if he were a drill sergeant giving orders to a new private. The execution of his words brought me to the heights of orgasm and he consumed every drop of my essence, leaving nothing behind but traces of the moisture his tongue produced.

"Hmm. Breakfast was delicious, baby." He stands to his feet and pulls me to a sitting position before helping me down from the countertop. He pulls my robe closed and ties the sash loosely. A little unsteady from the release, he holds me up until he's sure my legs are fully operating. I lean into him and wrap my arms around his waist.

"How do you always do that? I swear you give a whole new meaning to the word quickie." I speak into his chest.

"Baby, you just do something to me. I can't get enough of you. It's been that way since the first time I tasted you all those years ago. And it's only gotten deeper as the years have passed by. You are my only true weakness." He kisses the top of my head. "Are you ok?"

"Give me a minute." We both chuckle and stand in the kitchen holding each other until I reassure him that I am steady.

"Ok love. I'm going back upstairs to wash my face and brush my teeth before I head out. Are you ok?" he steps away slightly but stays close enough just in case he needs to prevent me from falling.

"Yes honey, I'm fine." I fix the sash on my robe. "Are you working late today?"

"No. No surgeries today. Just consultation visits and I meet with the accounting office later. It's tax time."

"Ok. I won't be late either. Maybe I can have Olivia prepare something special for dinner tonight?"

"That sounds great love. A quiet night in with you is just what I need."

"Sounds like a date."

"Indeed." He leans in to kiss me again. "I love you."

"I love you too." I watch him walk away towards the foyer to go upstairs. "Thank you, Lord, for such a good man."

Chapter Five

The driver arrives at the Michelle Obama Essence Gallery at 11:30 am. Thankfully there was light traffic on our route. We just missed the lunchtime rush hour through the city. Cassandra and I walk into the luncheon and check-in with the ladies at the reception table.

"Good morning Ms. McCray and Ms. Ramaro. Thank you both for attending the luncheon today. Ms. McCray, congratulations on your nomination this year. The work you have done in our community has been inspiring and your accomplishments this year in business have set records for your firm. Your nomination was well earned and deserved. You will be seated at table two with some of our other nominees. Here are your programs for today's event. The lunch buffet is open if you are ready to eat. There are also a variety of beverages and desserts at the tables along the back wall. If there is anything else you need or would like to request, please find one of our L.O.P. members and we will be happy to assist you." She extends her hand to shake ours.

"Thank you, Mrs. Pointer, it's truly our pleasure to attend. And I would like to thank your organization and members for the nomination. It was truly unexpected." I say and return the handshake gesture. Cassandra and I enter the dining room to locate our table. Each table round table seats eight people and there are at least thirty tables in the room. The place settings are labeled with name cards. Of course, being the first ones to arrive, we read the name cards to see who's at the table with us and look at each other. Cass laughs first.

"What the? Did they really put us at the table to these women?" Cassandra asks. "This is going to be fun."

"Come on Cass. We can't behave all ghetto like they expect us to. While we're here, we will be the professional women we are. No reason to give these snooty ass women a show they don't deserve or are looking for. Save everything you really want to say for the ride back to the office." I tap her on her side and we laugh quietly.

"You're right Lena. Just know that I will be keeping track of everything that happens today. I can feel the undercover shade in the room and I'm here for all of it. Let it begin." Cassandra laughed again. "Now come on. Let's go see what they have at this hoity-toity buffet. Is that lobster I see?"

Continuing our conversation, we select our plates and a set of silverware and make selections from the huge buffet. The Ladies of Pearl went all the way out for this feast too. There were servers standing behind the table to assist and explain what each selection was and every single dish looked amazing. With our plates full, we walk back to our table as more guests and nominees arrive. The women great each other and conversations begin to occur about different topics. The other tables fill up with people and the buffet line grows. Four ladies appear at our table and place their purses in their chairs.

"Hello, ladies." One woman says as takes off her jacket. "I'm Amaryss Davenport. I started the National Equality Organization for Women of Color. This is my business partner, Dorothy Hahn. We're both nominees for this year's Advocacy Award." Both women are well dressed in tailor-made women's suits and stiletto shoes. Before Cass or I can speak, I can tell they are making a mental note of us and sizing us up.

"Hello, Amaryss and Dorothy. I am Dalene McCray and this is my office manager and best friend Cassandra Ramaro. It's nice to meet you."

"And you as well," Dorothy replies. "are both of you ladies' nominees this year?" she asks in a snooty manner. I can smell the contempt coming off her as she stands across the table. My guess is the fact that we do not mention what or if we are nominees irritates her and that she must ask us is even more of an irritation.

"Lena is nominated this year for the Vanguard Award." Cass answers for me.

"Oh, and where do you work?" Amaryss asks.

I'm not sure what difference that makes but I decide to entertain her anyway. "We work at Jones, Jenkins, McCray & Associates."

"You're THAT D. McCray? I always thought that the D. Stood for Daryl or Dennis. It's a pleasure to meet you." Amaryss states. "To be honest, our company has been trying to get a meeting with your firm for months. Maybe this is kismet or just pure luck that we are at the same table." Dorothy looks around and switches the seating cards so she and Amaryss are sitting right next to us at the table.

"Stranger things have happened." I mention.

"Well, we'll be right back. We're going to get in the buffet line before it gets extremely long. It looks as if this will be a large crowd today for this event." Amaryss looks around at the sea of tables and chairs. "Do you have any suggestions from the table? Or can we bring you anything back?"

"Everything we had was pretty tasty. I don't think you can go wrong with whatever you select to have. I don't want anything else, thank you for the offer. Do you want anything else, Cassandra?"

"No, I'm fine, thank you." Cass looks at me and I can see in her eyes she is about to explode.

"Alright. We'd better get to it." They walk away and whisper to each other.

"Can you believe these heffas?" Cass asks and covers her mouth to keep her laugh muffled. "I knew who they were when they walked up. Acting as if they don't know who you are. Bihhh, please. I wanted to bust them out so bad."

"Not here Cass. But we will definitely talk about this on the ride back to the office." I say.

"Ok. But Jesus be a fence on a windy day, because only you can keep my mouth shut right now."

I laugh, knowing Cass is right but I need for her to hold on to her composure. It has and will never be my practice to allow anyone to feel like they caught me off guard. I'm always ready for the bullshit that people tend to spew when they think you are not looking. I search the room for more recognizable faces and see a few more ladies I've done business with. We exchange waves and mouth hello across the room to one another. From the looks of the crowd, as they arrive, this will be a great event with a lot of networking beyond the luncheon and awards. Even if I don't win the award, I will surely gain new clients in the end. I look at my watch to check the time and it's 12:10 pm. The awards presentation is scheduled to begin at 12:45 pm. Cass and I settle into our seats a little more and wait for the remaining members of our table.

Chapter Six

The clock on the wall says 11:45 am. I should be at the gallery by now but here I sit, in Dr. Mahoning's office waiting for her to come in with my test results. I arrived on time for my appointment at 10:00 am for my bloodwork. However, as I was leaving, her nurse came out and asked me if I could wait to speak with the doctor. I had plenty of time when she asked, however, now it's getting close to the start of my luncheon and I cannot late. I pick up my purse to leave and Dr. Mahoning enters her office.

"Mrs. Dane, my apologies for keeping you waiting. It has been an absolute, crazy day here. Normally, I would have been in to see you sooner."

"I was just about to leave Dr. Mahoning. I have an event I need that I am hosting and I cannot be late. I'm already late waiting here. Can we reschedule this for another day? I really need to get going."

"Again, I apologize for the wait." Dr. Mahoning apologizes again.

"Dr. Mahoning, I am a busy woman just as you are. I cannot spend my time waiting in your office half the day when I have things I am responsible for. I must leave as I have an engagement to attend. Please have your receptionist call me tomorrow to reschedule my appointment with you. I hope on that day, you will be able to see me in a timely manner. Good day." I snidely say and walk out of her office, not giving her a chance to rebuttal or persuade me to stay.

Outside of the doctor's office, I get into my car and leave the parking lot. The gallery is fifteen minutes away in light traffic. With the lunchtime rush, it will take me twenty-five minutes to get to there, which will make my arrival time 12:30 pm and the ceremony itself starts at 12:45 pm. I guess I will have to skip the buffet. I hate being late to anything, especially when I'm the person who organized the event. I change lanes several times to try and get through traffic faster. The clock in my car shows 12:27 pm and the longer the ride takes, the more pissed off I get. The radio is on and I turn the volume up a little more to get my mind off the traffic. After four lights, the traffic clears up and I'm able to make to the gallery by 12:40 pm. Instead of parking myself, I give my keys to the valet and I rush into the gallery.

"Zyera, where have you been? We didn't think you were going to make it. I called your cell several times but only got the voicemail." Mrs. Pointer says.

"I had an appointment and couldn't get to my phone. I would have been here sooner but I got held up. Anyhow, I'm here now. Let's get this party started." I say and enter the room filled with honored guests and community members. Gazing across the room, I notice the nominees seated at the front tables as they had been assigned. There are very few empty seats at the tables and I am proud to say this will be another sold-out event. The Ladies of Pearl have outdone themselves this year with me at the helm. This will be the most successful awards banquet to date and they have me to thank for it due to my connections in the community.

"Alright, it's go time." I say to myself and walk through the crowd of tables confidently to the podium at the front of the room. As I step up to the microphone, the room quiets as they realize the ceremony is about to begin. The sea of eyes all focus on me, with only a few still eating quietly or sipping their afternoon wine selection.

"Good afternoon nominees and guests. Welcome to the 2018 Exemplary Women in the Community luncheon. It is wonderful to see you all here today to celebrate not only this year's award winners but the nominees as well. The Ladies of Pearl organization has worked diligently to prepare for today's ceremony and celebration. As President, it is my pleasure to introduce this year's award winners. But first, in a change of tradition, the committee and I wanted to honor all this year's nominees for the works they have done in the community and their achievements in business. At this time, I would like all 30 of our nominees to stand. You ladies have made significant changes in our community by mentoring teen girls, volunteering in our community centers and homeless shelters, and creating campaigns to provide job training for women. You have also shown us that as women we can rule and win in boardrooms and courtrooms. I stand in awe of your fortitude, success, and should I dare say, that unstoppable girl magic!" The ladies stand and the room erupts with the sound of applause. All the nominees smile, while some bow and wave with their thanks. The applause continues for several minutes. "Thank you, ladies, for your contributions, your time, and your accomplishments." The nominees retake their seats. I continue through my prepared speech and lead to the awards. I watch and listen as each honored woman is gracious with her acceptance and inspiring with her speech of thanks.

After the final award, the Ladies of Pearl extended invitations for all nominees to consider joining the organization. Those in attendance today who wished to join were informed to meet with Mrs. Pointer before leaving for more information. In closing, L.O.P. member and Pastor Francine Gritch said a prayer to keep and cover us all as we continued through the remainder of our day.

"This was a great event Mrs. Danes. Thank you all again for the nomination and the award." Lena says and shakes Zyera's hand again. "Everything was amazing and the choice to have the event at this location was the icing on the cake. You and your organization continue to encourage women in this community to reach for every star they see without fear of failure. For that, I thank you."

"Ms. McCray, it has been my pleasure to serve with the Ladies of Pearl. I look forward to this event every year. Not only does it motivate women like you, it motivates women like me as well. Even though I am older than all the women honored today, you ladies provide hope for the next generation of professional women. That is what we need more of. More positive role models for our young women to model themselves after. When I was a young woman, there weren't many women in the professional world I could look up to but that has changed over the last thirty decades. That needs and should be recognized. And this organization is dedicated to making sure that happens." Zyera says with great pride.

"I know I for one am appreciative that the hard work we contribute to this community is recognized. I'm sure all the women who attended today either by nomination, association, and donation believe the same thing and feel the same way." Lena smiles and extends her hand for a farewell handshake. "Thank you again for this honor and I look forward to working with the Ladies of Pearl in the future."

"I look forward to it as well. Have a beautiful day Ms. McCray."

"And you as well Mrs. Dane."

The two ladies shake hands and part ways for now. Both speaking of working together soon, not knowing when that will be, however, knowing that it will come to pass. Lena and Cass leave the gallery and wait at the front door for the car to pull up. More women from the event exit the gallery as well. Each group carrying on their own conversations, laughing and congratulating each other as they pass by. Some of the other awardees pause to give their congratulations to Lena as well. Fake smiles are evident and it's clear the upcoming conversation to be had between the two friends will be full of shade and laughter. Looking at one another, they laugh without the need of one word. The car arrives and the driver gets out to open the doors ushering Lena and Cass inside. Once the door closes, they again look at each other.

"Girl, those bitches were full of cold cash shit. I can't believe the two from the table tried to act like they didn't know you. I remember when they contacted me inquiring if they could make an appointment to meet with you. Then get to the event and pretend like she didn't know you were a woman. Bihhh, get the fuck outta here!" Cassandra says and laughs.

"I already knew she was going to act like that. People think we forget. When will they learn? We never forget."

"That's exactly why her funky ass didn't win." Cass laughs harder causing me to laugh as well.

"What did you think about Zyera Dane though? Do you think she's as refined as she puts out?"

"I don't know Cass. But I do know she ain't no joke. The way she walked up in there today demanding the respect of the ladies from that organization. Yes, she's the truth. I can't even front or throw shade. There is something about her that speaks not only money but power as well. That's the kind of power that gets shit done without the need for a raised tone. That's the power that I want. I think we can learn some things from her and I hope we do get to work with her."

"True. Let me be clear Sis, you have power. The way you come through each day and make sure shit gets done. No questions, no doubts, and no damn concerns. You know I'm your biggest fan and greatest supporter. Even if you had never hired me to be your personal assistant, I would be in your corner. That shit is real."

"I know Cass. You are not only my most trusted friend, you are family. And we both know that family is not always determined by blood."

"You know I got you. Straight up, no chaser. You go, I go. You ride, I ride."

"And you know I feel the same way about you, Sis." We share a look that reflects our twenty plus years of sistership.

"Alright enough of all this mushy shit. To the shade! Cass, did you see the lady in the yellow hat?" I throw my head back and laugh.

"Yes Bihhh, she looked like she was going to Easter service instead of a luncheon. Who told her to wear that ugly dress with those shoes? She knew better than that. I know she did!" Cass says and joins me with a laugh. For the remainder of the ride back to the office, we talk about what people wore, how much they ate, and even some of the speeches. This conversation is exactly what I need. Cass always knows what to say and what to do. We arrive back at the Concorde Building before my last meeting of the day. Back to business.

Chapter Seven

Maleek parks his car in the parking lot of Horns Lounge and walks around to open my door like a true gentleman. Offering his hand, he helps me out and closes the car door behind me, then locks the doors by the remote. Surprisingly, he grabs my hand and we walk toward the entrance.

"Have you ever been here before little girl?"

"Little girl? Why would you call me that?"

"I don't mean anything by it. I'm not trying to insult you, sweetheart. It's just a nickname."

"Oh. No, I've never been here before. I've been hearing about this place for a few weeks though. Heard they have this amazing singer that is setting the streets on fire."

"Yeah, she's pretty good. Before you ask, I've never escorted another woman here. I've been saving that for you. I wasn't sure if you'd been here before, but I knew that I didn't want to share this place with another woman. I have every intention of making this our place."

"Our place huh? And what makes you think we're going to have date number two?"

"Confidence for one. For two, the fact that you've been checkin for me for the past two months. Yeah, I noticed. I didn't say anything and wasn't going to say anything until I knew you were ready."

"Hmmm. From what I can tell, you were checkin for me too. You think I didn't notice you watchin my ass when I you were supposed to be training me?"

"I was watching your form. That's my job."

"Watching my form? Yeah ok. If that's what you need to tell yourself."

"It's the truth. I didn't say I didn't like what I saw. Besides, if I was going to ask you out, I had to make sure that body was right. You're a product of my brand."

"Yeah ok. Whatever you say."

"Miracle." We stop before entering the building. "You know I'm just messing with you right now. I was checkin you, damn girl, who wouldn't be. A man would have to be blind to miss seeing you in any room. But I'm not the kind of dude to stress no woman out or even put myself in a position of vulnerability. I don't have to. Women come after me normally. But there's something about you that has me interested enough to shoot my shot."

"I get it Maleek. You're not the first one to come after me because of my V card and you won't be the last. I'm a challenge. Don't trip though. I'm not innocent by any means, I just haven't traveled that road and I don't plan to until I'm ready. So, if you're in this to do something no one else has been able to do, you're wasting your time."

"Damn girl, didn't I just tell you I'm not in it for that. We're going in here to listen to some live music, have a few drinks, and enjoy the evening. Ok?"

"Ok." I reply. He leans in to kiss me softly.

"Ok. Now let's go have a great time."

We enter the lounge still holding hands. Maleek pays the cover charge and we are shown to a table in the VIP section behind a cream-colored rope. There are couple styled sofas with small round table in front of them. There are tablets at each love sofa to place drink orders directly to the bar and food orders directly to the kitchen. The middle set has a "Reserved" sign on the table and that's exactly where Maleek took me to sit. I'll admit, it impressed me that he took the time to arrange all of this for me.

"I see you went all out for little old me." I touch my hand to my chest. "Seems like you like me a lot." I laugh and touch his chest.

"Only the best for you little girl. You don't know me or who I really am. I'm more than a personal trainer. I'm more than this face and this body. If you stick around, you just might get to see every side of me." He touches my chin and leans in again for a kiss. The band is playing covers softly as the club begins to fill up. Maleek picks up the tablet. "What are you drinking?"

"A glass of white wine would be great. Thank you."

"I gotchu. Are you hungry? I'm going to order a couple appetizers to munch on."

"Whatever you order is fine." I turn to watch the band while he places the order for drinks and food. It's Saturday night and the room begins to fill up with patrons. I love how the crowd is mixed with all kinds of people from different cultures and races. The vibe in the room was already poppin and the night was just getting started.

"Why did you do that?" I ask Maleek.

"Why did I do what?" He settles back into the love sofa and places his arm around me.

"Why did you do all of that and say all of that stuff in the gym? Did you know that you were going to ask me out and that we would be here tonight?" I look into his eyes. We're sitting so close I can feel his breath when he exhales.

"You're looking at me all innocent with those brown eyes. Like a newborn puppy in a pet store hoping to get adopted. You are so beautiful. I know you've used that beauty to get you in things and out of things. I told you, I've been watching you for months. Waiting to see when or if you were interested in me. I know I'm a good lookin dude and I can have my pick of women on any day. I get approached and asked out and all that shit. But that doesn't entice me. I'm an alpha male all day. I enjoy the chase and the challenge. Most women think that baggin a man is easy. It's only easy because most dudes only wanna fuck. I'm not like that. I've never been like that. That whole scene in the gym was needed to break the ice. That's me chasin you girl. Let me chase you, damn. Or is that a problem?"

I can tell he's being honest. Even with the club reaching capacity, it still feels like we're the only two in the place. Our drinks and food arrive and the waitress places everything on the table in front of us. Maleek tips her and hands me my glass of wine then picks up his own drink.

"Is that a problem?" He asks me again.

"No, it's not a problem." I answer.

"Then sit yo fine ass back, drink that white wine, enjoy these appetizers, and get ready to listen to some good music. The girl who sings here on the weekends will be on stage soon. Her voice is amazing."

I sit back and place myself in the crook of his body. Feels like I'm the missing piece to his puzzle as I snuggle in and pulls me in close from behind.

I view the floor below and almost all the seats are filled with people and there is still a line at the door hoping people leave. Another couple joins us in the VIP section. The woman and I mouth hello while Maleek and man exchange the proverbial, "what's up bruh." Maleek and I chat and he kisses my cheek in between verbal exchanges in our conversation. I am having a great night so far. I can only hope it gets better.

The lights dim and a spotlight is concentrated on the microphone on stage. A man walks on stage from behind the side curtain and the crowd offers an applause.

"Hello, hello, hello my people. I'm Michael and I want to welcome you to Horns Lounge. It is amazing to see all the beautiful people in here tonight. If this is your first time here, thank you for coming through. I'm sure it won't be your last cuz we keep it hot and poppin up in here. How are the drinks and the food? Not only are we the best night spot for the grown and sexy six nights a week, we also have the best bartenders and kitchen team in town. Make sure you drink up and tip CT and Banks well. Those brothers are working hard for you back there at the bar. Treat them well and they'll do the same. And don't forget about your waitresses. Tonight, we have Shan, Danielle, Reesie, Silver, and Stacey working the room taking orders for the bar and the kitchen. Hey ladies!" Michael waves at the bartenders and the waitresses who are all stationed at the bar. This allows him to have the full attention of the room.

"As we do every Saturday night, we are going to bless your ears with the angelic vocals of Horns' own Kamryn Slade and our house band Soulful Sounds." The crowd erupts with whistles, applause, and cheers. "Yes. Horns is lucky as shit to have her here and we know it. She gives her all on our little stage and tonight she is here to give you butterflies in your stomach and goosebumps down your arms. Are you ready to hear my girl?" The crowd sounds off confirming what Michael already knew. "Alright then, let's get this night started. Put your hands together and welcome to the stage, Kamryn Slade." Another loud applause fills the air as Kamryn makes her way to the stage.

"Thank you! Thank you! Wow, thank you all for coming out tonight. And thank you even more for the love. What do you think, do you want to get right into it?"

"Yes!" The crowd says.

"Alright Soulful Sounds, let's give the people what they want." The room claps and cheers as the band begins with a guitar intro. "Ladies, have you ever felt like you had to pretend to be someone you're not? Don't we all just want that man in our lives to love us for who we are? No extra shit. No additions that didn't come with the original package. I don't know about y'all, but I want my man to love me naked. Listen to the words of Ella Mai." I look back at the guitarist and the drummer adds a tapping beat. "Take away the big shirts, the tattoos, the sweatpants, and Vans. Okay, I don't wear no makeup, no purse in my hands. My resting bitch face is mistaken for the mean girl. But what if I told you, there's nothing I want more in this world than somebody, who loves me naked. Someone who never asks for love but knows how to take it. Are you that somebody who sees a wall and breaks it. Are you ready to fight just to see what's lost behind my flaws? Can you love me naked? Yeah, yeah, yeah, yeah."

The crowd sways to the soft beat and some women look at each other as Kamryn sings the words. Clearly, women in the crowd understand what she's saying and nod their heads in sisterhood and agreement. This song is touching the soul of people in the room and everyone is loving the performance. Michael looks on from off stage and stares at Kamryn knowing she is in her zone. The lights bounce off her free-flowing honey blond locks create a halo around her head. He walks off stage to view the stage from the floor.

"Damn this girl can sing." Says a man sitting at the front table. The woman he's with nods her head and they both turn back to the stage to enjoy the show.

As Kamryn goes into the next verse of the song and then the bridge, Michael scans the room for reactions to her vocal abilities. It's hard to believe a woman so young has such untapped talent. Horns Lounge is lucky to have found her and even luckier that no one else has discovered her yet. But Michael has a feeling that will change soon. In a few weeks, music producers and DJs are going to be in the city for an award show at the theatre and it's a good chance that some of them will come through Horns. Kamryn's videos on Horns social media page have sparks thousands of views and he's already been contacted asking for her information. It's only a matter of time.

The rest of the night was filled with amazing vocal selections from Kamryn. She kept the crowd thoroughly entertained with cover selections from artists across the age and gender spectrum to include Jazmine Sullivan, Alina Baraz, Betty Wright, Lalah Hathaway, Sam Smith, Aaliyah, and Fantasia. The medley of songs she sang, rang out into the streets as passers-by paused and peered in the door of the lounge trying to see who was singing. Cell phones aimed towards the stage recording or live streaming this young song bird's talent will reach hundreds before the end of the night. Maleek and Miracle sat in each other's arms all night, enjoying each other and this perfect night.

The last song of the evening was a favorite of Miracle's. Kamryn grabs the microphone. "Did you all have a great time tonight?" The crowd replies with cheers. "I'm glad you did. I know I had an incredible night too and that is because of you all out there. I can't say thank you enough for your support and encouragement. Your energy gave me energy. That's what I call a fair exchange. To show my appreciation, my final song of the night is Heaven by Justine Skye. If you know the words, sing along. I saved this song for last because this is exactly what you make me feel like when I'm up here." With her last words, the music starts and Kamryn bounces with the beat. "Who ever said you need a halo, to make it out alive."

As Kamryn sings the words, Miracle sings along with her from the VIP section. Maleek can hear her and looks down at her. For him, as he listened to the words, he realized that it absolutely explained how he was feeling right now.

44

Seems like this was a great night not just for Kamryn on stage and Michael with his business. But it was a great night as well for Maleek and Miracle.

Maleek and Miracle sit in the VIP section as the other patrons empty the club and filter outside. "Did you have a good time little girl?"

"I had a great time. Thank you for bringing me here. This was a wonderful first date. I love this place." She looks in his face again smiling.

"That was the plan. I told you already, this is going to be our spot. I knew you would love it." He touches the tip of her nose and smiles back at her.

"Very calculated huh? You do know you're not slick and this is not going to make me let you in my panties right."

"That was never a part of my plan. I didn't bring you here to loosen you up with drinks and take advantage of you Miracle. I brought you here to show you, I'm not what you think and more than what you know." He rises from the love sofa and reaches for her hand to assist her. "Let's go. It's getting late and I want to get you home and out of these streets."

"Alright." Is all she says as she allows him to lead her through the lounge and out the building. When they get to his car, he unlocks the door with the remote and opens the door for her. Once secured inside, he closes the door and walks around to the driver's side. The drive to her home is quiet with the volume of the radio down low. Maleek pulls onto Miracle's street and soon is in her driveway. "I had fun Maleek truly. It was different than what I expected from you."

"What did you expect? The drive-thru for dinner or Netflix and chill?"

"I wasn't sure but I wanted to give you the opportunity to show and prove. I'm glad you went beyond my expectations."

"Oh, you ain't seen nothing yet." Before she could reply, Maleek has exited the car and walked around to open her door. "Come on, let me make sure you get in the house safe." He takes her hand and walks her to her front door.

Miracle unlocks the door but does not open it to enter the house. She turns around and looks at Maleek. "Thank you again. I had a great night."

"You're welcome Miracle." He grabs her in his arms and kisses her softly. When he releases her he looks into her eyes. "Now get in the house, I'll call you tomorrow." He turns her around and steps back. Closing the door, Miracle looks out the side window to see Maleek get in his car, back out of the driveway, and drive away.

"Am I that lucky to find someone so perfect?"

Chapter Eight

Waking up to the sound of birds chirping is peaceful and serene. That's one of the things I love about being at Michael's. I look over and see him soundly sleeping. Damn, he is fine. I touch his face with the back of my hand and run my fingers across his beard. Yes honey, beard game matters. Turning over on my side, I move closer to him and listen to his steady breathing. That too is peaceful.

I've been seeing him for almost a year. Never met his parents. I don't even know if they're alive. I don't know if he has siblings or any family at all. But that doesn't bother me as much as realizing that I've fallen for him. Looking at him, I know I can wake-up every morning in this same spot, doing this same thing, feeling this same way. I love him. I'm in love with him. That feeling scares me but raises my heart rate at the same time.

"I'm in love with you." I whisper and search his face for a signal that he's awake or that he heard me but nothing happens. I let out the breath I've been holding in relief and close my eyes.

"I know." His voice says. I open my eyes to see him staring at me. "I'm in love with you too. I've been waiting for you to realize your feelings. I've known for a while." He raises his hand to my face and strokes my cheek.

A tear forms in my eye and falls. He wipes it away. "I'm scared." I admit. "I'm scared that this is not real. Is it?"

"It's real Lena. It's as real as it can be without it being a dream." He moves closer to me, rolling me onto my back, parting my legs, and placing himself in between them. I instinctively raise my knees to give him access to what he wants. Posted above me, he gazes into my eyes. "Is this real enough for you?" He enters me smoothly and watches as the feeling of ecstasy is read across my face. Our eyes remain connected as he gives me doses of him while he pumps in and out of my body. We are one at this moment, more than we've ever been. He slides his left hand down the side of my body until he reaches the backside of my thigh, raising it to place it on his shoulder.

"How real is it now?" he asks me and plunges deeper into my chamber of passion. "Do you think this is a dream, my love? Do you not trust what you see, what you feel, what you hear?" he strokes deeper and faster. "Tell me. Tell me what you feel right now."

"I can't." Is all I can say. "I can't."

"Yes, you can. Tell me." He says. He lowers his mouth and tastes my nipple as if it were the for the first time. "Tell me. If you love me the way I know you do, part your lips and tell me." He says in between sucking and nibbling on my nipple. "I want to hear you. I need to hear you."

"I can't."

"Dammit woman, what do you need? Do you need me to say what I feel? Do you need to hear me?"

"Yes."

He withdraws his dick and begins to lower his body, placing kisses down the middle of my abdomen along the way. He reaches the place that brings every woman to tears and every man to his knees. I look down my body at him as he stares at her silently. He raises his eyes to meet mine.

"Lena, you are the love I've waited my life for. The one who has captured my heart and my body. I am yours to do with what you will. Even if this confession drives you away from me, it is what I need to say and what you need to know. I am yours, Lena. Now and forever. What else do you want?"

"Nothing." Is my only response. I place my hands on the back of his head and guide him to the head of my pussy. His mouth opens instinctively as he latches on to me again making us one. His tongue dances with my clitoris like two lovers doing the tango. A dance of desire and hunger from one lover to another. Capturing it within his lips, making it summersault and vibrate as I shake with pleasure. My grip on his head tightens as I feel my climax begin to climb. The rush of heat starts to overtake me and my breathing picks up its pace. "Oh, gawd. Michael. Ahh." I let out.

He pauses, "What do you feel? What do you want?"

"You. I want you, baby. Only you." I manage to whisper.

"You want me? Are you sure?" He penetrates my sweet spot with his tongue.

"Yes, baby. Ohhhhh. Yes."

"Do you only want me for now?" He says while placing soft wet on the insides of my thighs.

"I want you forever." I say in a moan that is barely auditory.

"Marry me." Michael says as my orgasm sits at the peak of the ledge. "Will you marry me?" Sensing my climax, he takes my clit in his mouth, sucking as if I am the last meal he will ever have.

My orgasm spills out of me as my body jerks with convulsions I've never experienced before. A tear falls from my eye. "Yes!" I answer him while he swallows every ounce of what escapes me. "Yes, baby." He raises the full length of his body to match mine. He enters me again with fever and lust driving his body into mine.

"Are you sure you want to marry me? Once I put that ring on your finger, this pussy belongs to me and I will have no mercy." He stops and flips me over putting me in the position I love the most. He slaps my ass, "Now give me that deep arch I like to see." Then places himself behind me on his knees. Hands on my hips, he feels me up in one move. "Ahhh, yes!" His head falls back as my walls contract and release.

I moan and fall into his rhythm, giving back to him what he is giving to me, catching what he is throwing and relishing every minute of it. His hand moves to grip my shoulder to gain more leverage and force. Then runs down the center of back giving me visible shivers.

"Don't shake and don't run. Give me what I want. Give me what's mine. Keep throwing that ass back and I want to hear you." He says as he slaps my ass again.

I moan and he pumps faster. I can tell from his speed and his breathing, he's close to his own orgasm. "Cum for me baby." I plead with him. I know he's holding back for me, to make this session last longer. "I'm ready baby. I'm ready." I reach back and touch his hand that is resting on my hip. Grabbing hold,

I bring it around to play with my clit. My finger on top of his. We both make small circles, stimulating me, and bring me to another orgasm so we can cum together.

"No, not yet. I'm not ready. Shit!" He under cups my shoulder and lays his chest on my back as his body prepares to expel his seeds. The faster he pumps into me, the tighter he holds on. "I can't hold on baby. Ahhh! Lena, I'm cumin!" He moans and releases his seeds of life inside of my body. We fall onto the bed in exhaustion as he pulls me close to him. Feels like he's trying to meld my body into his so we remain as one person. One heart, one spirit, one body.

As we lay together still intertwined, there is only the sound of us breathing in the room and the birds chirping outside the window. He snuggles his head into my neck from behind. Soon his body relaxes but his hold does not. I place my hand on top of his as he rests. Before I close my eyes, my mind realizes that this is the first time we've ever made love without protection.

Chapter Nine

Eric hadn't been to Horns since it's opening night five years ago. The place has gotten better over time with the expansion of the VIP area and the new stage. This was a great investment to make and was bringing in money hand over fist. When James, his investment consultant, brought him the business plan, he wasn't sure. But James was convincing and made valid points regarding the plan. From the looks of business and after reviewing the accounting books, Eric was glad he had listened to him.

The view from VIP is astonishing. Eric can see everything from the stage to the front door by turning his head from left to right. He observes the crowd and notices someone sitting by one of the stage spotlights. Her face looks familiar. For the first time in his life, he doesn't trust his own eyes. Eric leaves the VIP section venturing down by the stage for a closer look. Are his eyes playing tricks on him? Could this really be Helen? It's been twenty years since he's seen her. Her eyes are fixed on the stage as Soulful Sounds plays softly and doesn't notice him walk up and sit near her.

"Hey, stranger." Eric says.

Even with the music, there is no mistaking that voice. She turns and looks right into the green eyes of her past. "Eric Danes." She says slowly.

"In the flesh. Wow! Helen Slade. How long has it been?"

"Twenty-two years."

"You haven't aged one bit. Honestly, you look better. Sexier. I guess it is true what they say. Black indeed does not crack. What brings you to Horns?" He stares at her intently.

"Thank you for the compliment, Eric. If that's what you meant it to be. If you must know, I came to watch my daughter perform."

"Watch your daughter perform? Kamryn is your daughter?" He asks, now very intrigued by the conversation.

"Yes, she is. Wait, how do you know her name?"

"My son has been telling me about this talented singer he hired. I

51

thought it was time for me to come by and to check her out for myself. And just think, if I hadn't come tonight, I would've missed this reunion. When did you get married?"

"He hired? Your son owns Horns? Kamryn told me the owner's name is Michael Ali. And to be clear, this is not a reunion. I didn't get married. But I'm guessing you still are."

"Yes, my dear, Michael is my son. My boys decided to use their middle name and my wife's maiden name for professional reasons. They wanted to be taken seriously in whatever they decided to do without the last name Dane attached. Wanted to make it on their own. I'm just a silent partner in their businesses."

"You don't look too silent tonight." She says as the lights dim signaling the start of the show. They both turn their attention to the stage.

Like every night, Michael makes his appearance on stage to give his greeting and thanks, t hen welcomes Kamryn to the stage. The crowd cheers and Helen smiles at the love her daughter is receiving from the crowd. Kamryn follows her nightly routine, speaking to the crowd first to get them warmed up. Beginning her set, she falls into her trance. Her voice flows through the speakers effortlessly as she sings to the crowd.

"Helen, she's beautiful." He leans in close and says. "Just like her mother."

"Thank you, Eric. You know, if you look closely you can see the blonde in her hair. Just like her father." Helen says. She can feel Eric's eyes on the back of her head. "When she was born, her eyes were green but by the time she was two, they changed to brown."

Eric feels like he's just taken a gut shot and all the wind's been knocked out of him. "What? What did you say?" Helen turns back to Eric. The look in his eyes is a look of confusion and disbelief. "What are you saying?"

"You heard me. Congratulations Daddy." She turns back to the stage to watch Kamryn. "It's a girl."

Eric stares at Helen with shock and dismay. Then he looks up at

Kamryn. That's my daughter? Oh God, what have I done?

Chapter Ten

After dating Maleek for six months, I finally agreed to let him cook me dinner at his townhouse. Not that I don't trust his cooking. More about me not trusting myself with him unchaperoned. The last six months have been amazing with him. No pressure, no promises, and no regrets. I didn't think something like that was possible when dating. Most dudes lose interest after two months of not getting anywhere with me, but Maleek is different.

"It smells good in here. What are we having?" I ask as I walk into his kitchen. I pick up the lid of a big pot on the stove and pops my hand.

"Mind your damn business, little girl and get out of my pots. Didn't your mama ever tell you not to lift another person's lid off their food? Have a seat over there." He points to the barstools against the waist-high countertop. I turn to walk over and he slaps my ass.

"Sorry." I say and laugh as I take a seat as ordered. "It smells delicious so I know you didn't cook it yourself. What did you do? Order delivery before I got here and throw the packaging away?" I laugh again.

"No, I did not. Trickery is not my forte in any form, shape, or fashion little girl. I cooked this food myself. Just a little something my mama taught me before I left the house to be on my own. A brother can cook, clean, do laundry, and take damn good care of myself and you, if you'd let me."

"I don't need you to take care of me. I can take care of myself. Or haven't you already noticed that?"

"Oh shit, I notice a lot of things. More than you think and more than you know. It's you who needs to open her eyes and see what she has in front of her. Or else it will pass you by. A brother ain't gone wait forever for you to notice what others already see."

"Well, a brother needs to realize that I am the prize. And the fact that I know that is proof in point that I realize my own worth."

"Little girl, a brother does notice that too. Just like a brother noticed you walked up in my house and didn't give me a kiss?" He leans over the counter.

"My fault. The smell from the kitchen got me excited. You know how I love food. And whatever you're cooking is making my mouth water."

"At least I know something gets you excited. Damn, I should have invited you over a long time ago." He laughs.

"You're not funny." I turn my head away from him and look around the room. "Your place is beautiful. I love the artwork. I didn't expect this type of décor, I thought you'd have half naked women on the wall, a pool table, big flat screens in every room, and a full weight set in your front room."

"What do you think I am? I'm not a playa little girl. And I'm not just some street dude who does personal training so I can feel on women. It's a perk of the job though." Maleek laughs at his own words.

"I never said you were a playa. I'm just surprised, that's all. I've never met a dude like you and you seem to be perfect. That's what scares me the most. Not too around here that would spend all the time you've been spending with me and not try to pressure me to give up the cookie. What are you trying to do? Get me all secure and feeling safe, then ambush me one night?"

"That's not my thing Miracle. If it was just about sex, I can get that without question. I don't know how many times I have to say that before you really trust me. It's not about that with you. I think you're a dope ass woman and I want to get to really know you. I want to know your mind, your spirit, your deepest goals, your most sacred loves, and all things about you that you don't share with anyone else. That's the dude I am. It's not about all that physical shit. Don't get me wrong, I want to see how that body feels under me, but I'm not in a rush. We have time for all that. Now come here and hand me that ladle." Miracle walks back in to the kitchen and grabs the spoon. "Don't sit down. Look in the cabinet by the fridge and grab two bowls. We're having seafood gumbo and it's spicy, so get two bottles of water out of the fridge."

"Yes sir." She says and gives him a salute.

"Keep it up and you're going to get a spanking." They share a laugh and sit down for dinner. The conversation runs through the meal and they enjoy each other's company. There never seems to be a lack of topics for them to cover and discuss. Being with Maleek is becoming Miracles favorite past time and she is not complaining about it, at all. They finish the gumbo and cornbread carrying their bowls to the sink.

"I wash and you dry." She says and turns the water on.

"I have a dishwasher. We don't have to hand wash the dishes."

"I know." Miracle grabs the scrub brush and the bowls. "Let's go. Get your sexy ass over here so we can watch these dishes. Then maybe we can Netflix and chill."

"Oh, you wanna Netflix and chill with a brotha? Do you even know what that really means? Cuz you ain't 'chilled' with anyone before. And you not gone sit here and rub all up on me and get my dick hard and go home, then I have to jack my shit off so I can go to bed."

"Yes, I know what it means and I have no intentions of giving you anything, much less a hard dick."

"I'm just say little girl." Maleek says and walks over to help her watch the bowls and silverware.

"Dinner was great honey. I really enjoyed it."

"Oh, I'm honey now?"

"Is that a problem?" She hands him the first bowl to rinse and dry.

"Should it be? Sounds to me like you tryin to put a brotha on lock and that's a big step." He asks as he dries the bowl and reaches for the second one.

"Should it? Is that what it sounds like?"

"Why you keep answering my question with a question?"

"Why do you? I started the conversation."

"Ok, you got that." He laughs and slaps Miracle on the ass. "Yeah, it should be. You done?"

"I'll be finished in a minute. Go get the tv ready. Do you have any popcorn I can put in the microwave?"

"Yeah, there's some in the pantry."

"OK. I'll meet you on the sofa." She watches him leave the room with her gaze dropping to his ass. "Hmmm." The sound escapes her lips and she laughs lightly. "Is he for real?"

Chapter Eleven

"Thank you all for your love and support. I am truly humble and appreciative. Please enjoy the amazing Soulful Sounds and I'll be back twenty minutes." The crowd cheers for Kamryn as she leaves the stage for her break. Exiting the stage, she looks across the crowd and sitting behind the stage light is her Mom. Kamryn squeezes past people and tables to reach Helen. "Mom! What are you doing here?"

Helen stands to hug her daughter with tears in her eyes. "I wanted to surprise you baby. You've been talking about this place and I wanted to see what all the fuss was about. Now I know. All the fuss is about you. You are amazing baby. I am so very proud of you." Helen hugs her daughter again.

"Thanks Mom. I wish you would have told me you were coming. I would have put in a reservation for you in VIP. What time did you get here?" They sit down in the booth that Helen has been sitting in all night.

"I don't need that baby. Besides, then it wouldn't have been a surprise and I wouldn't have gotten to see you purely in your zone. I arrived fifteen minutes before you started singing. I waited in the car until you got here before I came in and sat down. I wanted to get here early enough to find a good seat but not too early that you would see me before you started singing."

"Mom, you've seen me perform before. This is nothing new."

"Baby, I've seen you perform in school and church choirs. This is different. This is just you baby. No back-up, no team, just you and your beautiful voice. I can't believe I doubted you. I apologize for being so cynical." Helen grabs Kamryn's face with her hands like she would do when Kam was little.

"Mom, you were doing what you thought was right for me. It's ok. There's no need for you to apologize. You're my Mom. I love you. And you're here!" She hugs her mother again.

Captivated with her mother and ecstatic about her being at her show, Kamryn doesn't see the gentleman who is sits a few feet away. He watches the pair talk, laugh, and hug during Kamryn's break and instantly regrets coming over to the booth. He also feels jealous and furious.

Eric's mind rattles off question after question incoherently. The voice in his mind makes a list of questions he will be asking Helen as soon as he can get her alone but he knows this is not the right time or place. Why didn't she call me when she found out she was pregnant? Why did she keep the baby when she was in nursing school? Why didn't she come to me for help? When was she born? How could she have kept this from me for twenty years? Why didn't I check on her over the years? Shit, if I were her, I wouldn't have told me either.

The first time I saw her, my dick got hard. I couldn't keep my eyes off her. The entire lecture, my eyes always made their way back to hers. I read her body language and she was pushing pure pheromones from her pores and they were going right up my damn nose. For weeks, I was trying to get into her panties so much, I almost forgot I was married and had three young kids at home. Twenty-three years ago, this beautiful woman sitting less than five feet away, was my kryptonite and tonight she proved she still is. In more ways than one. She was the one and only time I'd strayed during my marriage. And she gave me the one thing my wife didn't, a daughter. I have a damn daughter! Wait, I have a daughter. What am I going to tell my boys? What am I going to tell Zyera? How am I going to tell Zyera?

Kamryn is welcomed back to the stage by the crowd and gets right into the music. Eric sees this as his chance to get some answers and moves closer to Helen. "Now is not the time Eric. This is not the place for your questions or your words of I'm sorry. I'm enjoying my daughter sing for all these people who came here tonight to see her." Helen says without looking at him. "I'm in town for three nights. Those days and nights I will spend with my daughter. You and I can meet Sunday for lunch at Santino's and you can ask me all your damn questions. Now, back, the fuck, off!"

Eric leaves Helen in the booth. Instead of going back to VIP, he goes to Michael's office to think. How is he going to tell his family that twenty years ago, he had a child outside of his vows? How are his sons going to look at him knowing he cheated on their mother? How is he going to handle this situation with Helen and Kamryn? Kamryn. Wow. From what he can tell, she is amazing. Kamryn, his daughter, his baby girl. He's never been selective of what he had when it came to children. Girl or boy, it didn't matter, long as the child was healthy. That's all he ever cared about. Anger sets in, realizing Helen kept his only daughter away from him. If he hadn't have come here tonight, he would still be in the dark. He had a right to know about her. He had a right to watch her grow up. "Dammit Helen!" He screams.

Michael walks in on his father's tantrum. "Pop, what's wrong? Are you alright?"

"Sorry son. Yeah, yeah, I'm cool. Just got a phone call from someone at work." He says trying to   cover his tracks. "What's up?" They embrace as they always do.

"I saw you heading back here and wanted to know what you thought of Kamryn and her voice." Michael sits on the leather sofa in his office.

"Yeah, son. She's great. And beautiful too." Eric mentions and walks over to the small bar to pour himself a drink. "You want one?"

"Naw, I'm cool Pop. Yeah, she's both. I thought about trying to get her number and see what the deal with her. But she's young and I can't mix business with pleasure." Michael laughs lightly.

"Umm, no son, you can't mix business with pleasure. Especially not in this case." He sits on the sofa next to Michael.

"What does that mean Pop?"

"Just saying. This young woman is bringing in the crowd and making a name for herself and an even bigger name for your place. Keep your dick in your pants and keep it professional with her."

"Alright Pop. She's too young for me anyway. Kamryn's a sweet girl. All the fellas here look after her like a little sister. CT almost knocked some dude out a few weeks ago for grabbin her arm when she was bartending. I had to jump in and save him from a beatdown. Shit was funny as hell Pop."

"Glad you're lookin after her. I'm sure Helen will feel better knowing her daughter is safe and being watched over."

"Pop, who's Helen? That's the second time you've said that name in the last five minutes."

"Huh? No, I haven't."

"Yo, Pop. I know what I heard. Come on, tell me. Between me and you. You know I won't say anything to Ma." Michael coaxes his father to come clean. Or at least as clean as he wants to admit. "I saw you tonight. Talkin to that lady by the stage. Then I saw Kamryn go over to her after. Was that her Mom?"

"Yeah. That's her Mom."

"How do you know her?"

"I don't, saw she was fine, went over to see if I still got it. Your old man used to be something else back in the day. That's how I got your mother." Eric laughs nervously and slaps Michael on the leg.

"Pop. Come on. Tell me the truth. You already knew her before tonight huh?"

"Son, this is not the kind of conversation I should have with you."

"Pop, I'm not a little boy. I'm a grown ass man and I know chemistry when I see it. I could've done a whole science experiment about the sun off the heat that was coming from that booth. How do you know Kamryn's mother? Be straight with me. I'm your son and I love you, nothing you say will ever change that. What's up?"

"No woman could turn my head after I met your mother. She put me in a trance from the first day I saw her. I chased that woman down and would've slept on the stoop of her dorm if I had to. The day I married her, my whole world started over. Then you boys came along and I was complete. Then, ten years later, I met Helen. I was lecturing for a year at the college she was attending. I saw her and I almost tripped over my own damn feet. She was beautiful. She floated when she walked and I was under her spell. I had no intentions of cheating on your mother, and I'm not going to be a jackass and say that whole bullshit of, it just happened, I wanted it to happen. I wanted her. Your mother is my heart. But Helen was my kryptonite."

"Damn Pop, how long did it go on?"

"Seven months. But son, it felt like a lifetime. That woman made me feel like a king when I was with her, like I could do no wrong. I was a different man with her. I know that sounds bad but it never took away from my love for your mother or you boys. The funny thing is, I knew it wasn't going to last. I knew what it was and I knew what my reality was. She knew all about me and never once asked me for anything. But I gave her everything I could."

"Yo, Pop. That's crazy."

"Yeah, I know son. Seeing her tonight was not my plan. I had no idea Kamryn was her daughter until tonight." Eric avoids eye contact with Michael. His eyes stay glued to the floor instead.

"Did mom ever find out? Did she know about this woman?"

"No. Not that I know of anyway. When I thought she was close to finding out, I cut it off and walked away. Never looked back. Never contacted her again." In his head, he finishes his statement half-assed confession with, "Now I know that was a mistake."

"Pop. That's the past. It's done. Right?"

Eric continues to look at the floor, too ashamed to look at his son.

"Pop? It's over, right?"

"For the most part, yes. Seeing her tonight fucked me up though."

"Yeah, I can tell. Never seen you shook and tonight, you're shook. Like Scooby Doo, shook. If you weren't already white, I'd say you look like a ghost." Michael laughs at his joke.

"Just remember if I wasn't white, you would have that good curly hair." Eric laughs with his son.

"Now the hard question. Is Kamryn your daughter? You said you met her ten years after you and Mom got married, which I'm guessing is an estimated amount of time. Kamryn's twenty-one. Pop, look at me. I'm cool. Be honest with me about this. Is Kamryn my sister? I've never seen you shaken by anything but this has you messed up. Is she my little sister?"

"Son. I don't think we need to talk about this right now." He looks at his son. Unable to speak.

"Pop. Am I screaming? Am I hysterical? Do I sound pissed? No. You're my best friend. You always have been." Michael looks at his father. The man he's looked up to his entire life, his hero. The one who taught him how to read, write, and ride his first bike. He grabs his father's hand to offer him the support he needs right now to be brave.

"I'm sorry son. I'm so sorry. I swear, I didn't know Helen was pregnant. She never told me. She never contacted me. I never knew. I never knew I had a child out there in the world growing up without me, growing up without you and your brothers. I never fuckin knew." Eric falls back into the sofa as tears fall from his eyes.

Michael watches his father with sorrow in his heart. "Pop. You didn't know. Don't beat yourself up for that. That was Helen's choice not to tell you. Maybe she thought she was doing what was right for you. Maybe she didn't want to mess up what you had, shit I don't know. From this point forward, now that you do know, what are you going to do? Does Kamryn know?"

"No, she doesn't know who I am." Eric shakes his head.

"Are you going to tell her?"

"That's not my place son. That's for her mother to do. But if she does, I'll be here waiting for her."

"What do you want me to do?"

"Keep doing what you've already been doing. Don't change just because you know who she really is to us. Honestly, I'm glad that you can watch over her like a big brother is supposed to do."

"Pop, what about mom? What are you going to do about mom?"

"I haven't figured that out yet son. I'm scared as hell too. You know your mother is crazy."

"Yeah, I know Pop. I know. What about my brothers though. Can I tell them?"

"I don't want anyone else to know right now. I need to fully process this. FUCK!"

"Alright Pop, I got you. I got her covered too. I tell you one thing though. She's getting a damn raise. Can't be paying my lil sister what I've been paying her." Michael laughs.

Chapter Twelve

"The garden looks beautiful. Miguel and his team have done a wonderful job again this year getting it ready for spring. I can't wait for the roses to bloom by the gazebo. That is going to be the perfect spot for our summer family photos this year when Eric Jr and my grandkids come. We need new family photos with the whole family. Me, my boys, my grands, and you." Zyera says as she looks back at Eric. "What do you think?"

Caught-up in his own mind, Eric doesn't hear anything Zyera says. For the past two weeks, the only thing that keeps running through his mind is Kamryn. His talk with Helen didn't go as planned or at least not by his plan. He knew he couldn't strong arm her into answering his questions after all these years. All he wanted was to know why. Why didn't she tell him?

"Eric, did you hear me, where is your head at?"

"Sorry honey. Just, ummm, thinking about work. I have some new consultations scheduled this week for some reality stars during their off season and I'm just trying to figure out when I'll have the scheduled. What did you ask me?"

"I was talking about the gazebo and how we need new family photos."

"Oh, of course love. Whatever you want to do is fine, you already know that."

"I want to have a big family fourth of July party. Fireworks for the grands and all my boys here. No excuses. Make it happen." Zyera demands.

"Yo, Mom, Pop, where y'all at?"

"Evan! We're in the kitchen baby!" Zyera yells towards the front door. "Come here. I haven't seen you in weeks. Where have you been young man? What hot butt has you tied up away from me?"

"Ma, stop it, it's not like that. Nobody has me tied up anywhere. I've been working. You know I'm building my brand. I've been handling business." Evan says to Zyera as he hugs her and kisses her cheek. "Don't trip Ma. What's up Pop, how you feelin?"

"Hey baby boy. I'm good. Don't pay your mother no mind. You know she worries about her boys. Always a mother hen. What you doing out here?"

"Just came to check y'all out. Did Olivia cook anything for lunch. I'm hungry."

"Boy, get out of here." Zyera slaps her son on the shoulder, "I knew you didn't come all the way out here to get something to eat. What are you getting into today?"

"Nothin ma. Had a free day and wanted to come chill with Pop out by the pool. Enjoy this sun and this gorgeous day. What do you say Pop? Wanna chill with me today?"

"Sounds good son, I'll change my clothes and meet you outside." Before going upstairs, Eric kisses Zyera on the cheek and slaps her on the ass.

"Not in front of Evan." She swats her hand at him.

"That boy has me do that his whole life, it ain't nothin new. This is my house woman, you're lucky that's all I did." He slaps her ass again and proceeds upstairs to change.

"That man! Ugh!" She smiles anyway and turns to her son. "Evan, are you doing ok baby? Been eating right? Are you seeing someone special?"

"Ma, I'm good, trust me, ok? Of course, I'm taking care of myself. I'm eating well. Olivia gave me some recipes a while ago that I've been using and I have a team of nutritionists that work for me. I couldn't be in better hands."

"Ok. What about my last question? Are you seeing someone special?"

"I'm dating ma. You know me, I can't sit around for too long without some company and female attention. There's someone I'm trying to get close to. But she's strong ma. Not cutting me no slack and strong in who she is. She's cool. You'll like her."

"I'll like her, huh? When am I going to meet her?"

"When I'm ready ma. Don't push."

"Alright Evan. Don't make me wait too long. I have three grown sons and only two grandchildren. That needs to change soon before I'm too old to enjoy them. You and Edward are going to make me wait until I'm on my deathbed before you give me more. I worry about you two sometimes. Let me be clear, this is not my permission to go out here and make babies without being married, this is me saying I wish you would settle down and find a woman to love, who loves you in return. I'm not rushing you though." Zyera explains to her son. Grabbing his face, she kisses his cheek again. "Ok, enough of that. If you didn't bring swim trunks I believe you have some in your room upstairs. The pool house is open already and I had fresh towels put in there this morning. Something told me you were coming over today."

"Ma, you always know. Mother's intuition?"

"Boy, you come over the first hot day of the season every year since you moved out to hang out with your Daddy. Mama knows everything and forgets nothing." She kisses him again. "Leave the wet towels in the hamper in the pool house when you're done. I love you Evan and I'll see you later."

"Alright ma. See you later." He walks Zyera to the door, then goes to his room to change.

Father and son meet at the pool fifteen minutes later and spend the early afternoon swimming and catching up on the little things. After swimming for some time, they lay out on the loungers to dry off. Olivia brings out lemonade, bottled water, and lemon bars then returns to the house.

"Alright Pop, I need to talk to you about something."

"Awe shit. I knew this was too good to be true. What's going on?"

"It's nothing bad Pop, just want your advice. I've been dating this girl and yo Pop, I'm really digging her vibe. She's smart, independent, and funny. We have great conversations and can spend ours together without getting bored. We talk on the phone and make real plans. It's so easy hanging out with her. I'm trying not to mess it up. I want to invite her here to meet you and ma."

"Ok Evan. You said all of that and I don't hear anything negative. So, where's the problem?"

"Not sure how ma is going to react. She was just talkin to me about getting married and havin kids. I don't know if that's where this thing is goin, but I want to know what you both think about her because I'm ready to take it to the next level."

"Ok son. Your mother wants to have a big fourth of July celebration with the family to include family photos. EJ and his family will be here. Bring your friend and I'll have Edward bring the young lady he's dating too. All three of our boys together, your mother and I haven't had that in a while. And if your mama starts actin shitty or funny, I'll straighten her up. Everyone will be welcome." In his mind, Eric is wishing Kamryn could be here too.

"Thanks Pop. You always know what to do." Evan reaches across the lounger and fist bumps Eric. They lay out for another hour before they go in to shower and change. Its early evening by the time Evan leaves and head home. Zyera is still out with her ladies group.

The house is quiet giving him time to think about his lunch meeting with Helen last week. She told him, she was not going to tell Kamryn who he was. It broke Eric's heart hearing the words escape her lips. She asked him not to tell Kamryn either, especially since she was working in the club. Eric agreed under duress and heartbreak. When Helen asked if he had told anyone, she lied and said no. He knew Helen would find a reason for Kamryn to quit the club, if he had told her the truth about telling his son. He wasn't sure if she believed him but he stuck to the story. If Helen thought that he would let Kamryn walk out of his life before he really got to know her and she know who he was. Eric knows he needs a plan though and begins to construct it in his mind. Kamryn is going to know he her father is and who her brothers are. She has a right to know and to be rewarded like the boys.

Chapter Thirteen

Having her mom in town was so great. She hadn't realized how much she missed her until she was sitting there having breakfast with her and catching up. But there was something wrong. She noticed it that night after her performance but her mother just said she was tired from driving up to see her that day. Kamryn knows her mother and her moods as well as she knows her own and even though Helen wouldn't admit it, she knew something was going on. She didn't push though. She wanted to enjoy the time with her.

"We're almost done setting up Kamryn then we can start practice." The bandleader Lisa says.

"Ok. Whenever you're ready."

"Hi Kamryn." Michael says as he comes from the back of the club where his office is located.

"Hi Michael." She smiles at him.

"How's it going?"

"It's going well. Thank you again for the opportunity to sing here. And thank you for the raise." She laughs.

"Ha. You're welcome on both accounts. You've earned the raise. It's no secret the crowd comes in here Thursday through Saturday to hear you. Paying that cover charge, ordering drinks and food because of you. Not taking anything away from the bartenders and the cook, just stating the reality of it. Besides, it's the least I can do. You're family now. And we take care of family." He says looking her directly in her eyes. Staring at her face, he can see his father. Their father. Her brown eyes and hair texture are the same eyes as his Eric Jr. And they all have the same nose. He can't believe he never noticed it before. Even though they have different mothers, there is no denying the genetic code of Eric Dane. He smiles at her loving.

"Thank you, Michael. You all have welcomed me with open arms and made me feel like family. I can't thank you enough."

"Listen to me, you are family. No matter what you think. You are family. And because you are family, call me Edward. That's what my family calls me. Ok?" He takes her hands in his.

"Ok." Kamryn smiles wide.

Michael pulls her in for a hug and tears fill his eyes. His baby sister has been in his grasp for months and he didn't see it. As they embrace, he hopes the true and pure love he has for her seeps through his pores and into her spirit. Although he didn't get the chance to grow up with her, his love for her is real. Now, he must find a way to get her to feel it too. Before releasing her, he wipes the tears from his eyes then steps back.

"Alright girl. Back to practice, the band is waiting for you. I want you to have the best show of your life this weekend. I expect some producers and DJs to come through here all weekend. I made a few phone calls to some friends. You better get yourself ready to blow their minds."

"What! Are you serious? Oh, my, gawd!" Kamryn jumps up and down screaming as Michael stands there and watches his little sister enjoy the first present he's ever been able to give her. "Are you serious? Are you serious? Please be kidding. Do you think I'm ready for that? I've been saving money to pay for some studio time. I don't have a demo cd or anything."

"You don't need one. They are coming to hear you sing live. There's no demo better than your natural voice. You got this! Now, go practice!"

"Thank you, Michael, I mean Edward. Thank you so much. I promise to give it everything that I have all weekend. I only wish my mom would have waited until this weekend to visit. You are the best. Thank you!" She allows Michael to push her toward the stage to start practice with the band.

"Come on Kamryn. Let's get this started." Lisa says as the band finishes warming up. "Enough talking with the boss. We have work to do."

Michael smiles and walks back to his office, pulling out his phone. "Come on, pick up." After two more rings, the call is answered. He sits on the sofa and put his feet on the small coffee table.

"Hello?"

"Pop, where are you?"

"In my office, what's up son?"

"I contacted some friends in the music business and asked them to come check Kamryn out. They're all going to be in town this weekend because of the awards show and will be coming through Horns. Just wanted you to know."

"Thanks Michael. That's great to hear."

"You never told me what happened during the meeting with Helen. Apparently, she didn't tell Kamryn huh?"

"No son. She said she wasn't going to. Said there was no need because she's lived twenty-one years without knowing so why change that now. I don't like it. It pissed me the fuck off. Made me feel like my feelings don't matter at all. I don't know how long I'll be able not to talk to her myself. I want to get to know her. I want her to get to know me. I want her to know you and your brothers. This is bullshit but I don't know how to fix it or where to start to try."

"Well, I'm going to be her favorite brother for sure when she does find out." Michael laughs.

"Already making it a competition and your brothers have no idea." Eric laughs as well. "I'm glad you called too. Your mother is having a big bash for the family on the fourth of July. EJ and his crew are coming. Family photos and everything. She's in her feelings this year so let's make her happy. I'm going to need the points with this bomb I'm holding."

"We're holding." Michael corrected him.

"Yeah, we're holding. Evan is bringing his new girl and you bring yours. May as well get it all out in the open now."

"No problem Pop. Evan's bringing a girl? You remember what happened last time he brought somebody to meet ma right? Are you prepared for that? That shit was ugly."

"I remember and I already promised him I would keep a hold of her so that doesn't happen again."

"Sounds good but we know how she gets."

"I got this."

"Have you decided how you're going to tell Ma? That is going to be one hell of a conversation and I just want to make sure I'm as far away from that location as possible."

"Not yet. I'm trying to figure a lot of shit out right now. Between your mother and Kamryn, I don't know what to do. Either way, someone is going to be hurt. And that is what's going to kill me the most. Hurting the woman who has been by my side for thirty plus years and hurting my baby girl who I appear to have abandoned."

"You know I'm here Pop if you need me."

"I know son. This is something that's too heavy to carry alone. If I didn't have you to talk to about all of this, I'd go crazy." His office phone buzzes. "Hold on son. Yes Maria, what is it?"

"Your next consultation is waiting." Maria, his assistant, notifies him.

"Alright thank you. I'll be with them shortly." He ends the call with Maria. "I have to go son. Money to make, faces to fix, and titties to feel and push up."

Michael laughs, "Ok Pop. Love you man."

"Love you too."

Chapter Fourteen

"Hello?"

"What's up little girl?"

"Hey Maleek. Not much goin on with me right now. Just shuffling around the house doin some cleaning. You know, laundry and stuff. What's up with you?"

"On my way home from being out all day. I hadn't talked to you today so I am just checking on you. You eat yet?"

"Not yet. I'm going to make some chicken tacos after I finish cleaning. You eat?"

"No. But I'm about to eat some chicken tacos, as soon as my girl asks me to come over for dinner."

Miracle laughs. "Oh yeah?"

"Yeah."

"Do you wanna come over for tacos?"

"Well since you asked. I guess I can make my way over there." They both laugh over the phone at the other. "What time is dinner?"

"How about five?"

"Sounds good to me. I'll bring a bottle of wine since you're gonna feed a brotha. There's something I wanna talk to you about too."

"What do you mean? Is everything alright?"

"Yes, everything is fine. There's just something I wanna ask you. Don't worry. We can talk about it over the phone if you want to."

"I'm not worried." But she is.

"Stop it. Everything is good. Trust me." He can tell she's worried by her answer and the sound of her voice.

"Alright. See you later."

"Oh, for sure." Maleek disconnects the call as he pulls into his garage. How has he gotten to know her so well? And without the addition of sexual intimacy. It's exciting to wonder how he will feel if he ever breaches her wall of protection and be the first man to experience her love nest. His dick gets hard thinking about it. "Shit, let me take a cold shower first."

Maleek finishes his shower and checks the time. It's 4:15 pm. He looks through his wine stash and selects a bottle of red to go along with dinner. The music carries him to Miracle's in record time and before he knows it, he's on her front porch. She opens the door and immediately jumps in his arms. "Damn, this feels so good." He says to her and steps back.

"Yes, it does." She admits and steps aside to let him fully in the house. They walk back to the kitchen and he places the bottle of wine on the counter.

"Dinner is almost done." Miracle says. "Can you set the table? You know where everything is."

Maleek does as she asks as she finishes the chicken and warming the soft shells. The other ingredients for the tacos are already on the table, thanks to Maleek. She carries the platter with the chicken and shells to the table and they sit together. Maleek blesses the food and as usual they enjoy a happy and conversation filled dinner together. He decides to save what he wants to talk to her about until after they eat. As is their routine, they clean the dishes together then settle on the sofa to decide what to do for the remainder of the night.

Miracle didn't miss the fact that this thing Maleek wanted to talk to her about was not done during dinner. She can't take the suspense, so she jumps right in. "Ok, what do you want to talk to me about?"

"Patience is definitely not your strong suit huh?" Maleek laughs at his own joke. He places he hand on her thigh.

"Do I really need to answer that?"

"Not really, I was being a smart ass." He laughs again watching the frustration on her face. "You're cute when your mad."

"I'm not mad. I just want to know what you have to say and you're taking forever to say it."

"Alright, little girl, calm down. Since the first night we went out, I haven't dated anyone else. You have wrapped me around your finger without trying, without sex, and without any true commitment. Let me tell you something, that has never happened to me before. I find myself wanting to spend more time with you as the days go by and I don't want that to change. I don't know where your head is in all of this but I hope you wait until I finish to tell me your side of things. I know we're not officially anything, no titles, no commitments, no promises, but I want to be. And because I want to be, I want you to meet my parents. They are a big part of my life and you knowing them, will help you to know me better. Now, my mother is having a family fourth of July celebration and you have been invited. What do you say?" He exhales after saying all that in what seemed to be one breath.

"Ummm. Are you sure you want me to meet them?"

"After all I've said, you're really asking me that?"

"I'm just asking. I don't know if I'm ready for all of that. I mean, meeting parents is a big step and it means something when a man takes a woman to meet his mother. It means something."

"I know that Miracle. You mean something to me, actually, more than something."

"More than something?"

"Yes," he says and takes her hand. "a lot more than I expected. I thought that we would date a few times and that would be it. But the more time I spent with you, the more I began to see what a beautiful person you are on the inside, not just on the outside. Your laugh, your thoughts, your purity that is hard to find these days."

"I don't know what to say."

"Say you'll come with me and meet my mother."

Miracle looks at Maleek and searches his eyes for something, anything that shows he is not serious. The only thing she sees is the sincerity reflected that she hears in his voice.

"I love you Miracle. It took me some time to realize but I know in my heart it's real and true. I love you." Still holding Miracle's hand, he raises it to his mouth and kisses each finger, then takes her palm and places it against his cheek.

She still stares at him. Speechless and amazed at his words and his actions. Her beating in her ears and her stomach doing flips, she opens her mouth, "I love you too. I've never said that to anyone other than my parents and my Gram." She looks down at the floor. "I've never met anyone I wanted to say it to other than them. Until you."

"I'm not saying this to get in your panties, if that's what you're thinking. I'm saying this as a man to a woman."

"I didn't say it as an echo to your words. I said it because I mean it as well. Even though I'm scared to death as to what it really means, my heart and my spirit feel it."

He kisses her passionately and pulls her into his arms. She falls into him and returns the kiss pouring all the love she feels for him into their connection. They wrap their arms around each other and hold on for dear life, as if letting go will cause them both to fall off a cliff in the Grand Canyon. Each kiss sealing what they fell for each other in a way they have never experienced. A warmth in Miracle's body begins to burn from the bottom of her feet moving through her most sensitive places into her stomach and reaching the top of her head. Feeling as if the top of her head is about to explode. She grabs Maleek and slings to him as if he were the oxygen keeping her alive. Once the kiss is broken, they stare into each other's eyes searching for words or a sliver of direction in which they should proceed.

"Let's go to bed." Miracle says.

"Ok." Maleek agrees with little hesitation.

They move towards her bedroom slowly, with Miracle leading the way, as Maleek watches her ass from behind. Standing at the side of her bed, she begins to undress.

"Wait." Maleek stops her hands from pulling her t-shirt over her head. "Wait baby."

"Why?" She asks in an almost whiney tone.

"I want to wait a little longer."

"Why? I'm ready. I love you and I want to give myself to you."

"It's not that I don't want to be with you this way. It's not that I don't love you. I just want to wait. Just a little while longer, ok?"

"No. I'm ready." She begins to pull her shirt off again.

Maleek grabs her hands to stop them. "Miracle, listen to me for a minute. You have waited to find someone to give your most precious gift to. I am honored to be that person. I never thought I could stick with someone this long without having sex with them but I have. That means something special to me, probably more than it means to you." He raises his hand to touch her cheek. "Bae, you are more than just your body and I know that crossing this next line will not change how I feel about you but I want this to be different for me, not just for you. When I make love to you, it will be a night you remember for the rest of our lives. Do you understand?"

"Ok. We can wait." Not truly understanding but agreeing. Instead, she changes into boy shorts and a tank top while he pulls off his shorts and t-shirt, leaving only his boxer briefs on. They climb into bed and sleep in each other's arms as they have every night they spend together, whether at his house or hers.

"Good night love." Maleek says and closes his eyes, pulling her in tightly.

"Good night baby." She says in return, snuggling into him.

Chapter Fifteen

At points in life, we make the hardest decisions of our lives. The road we choose to take is the one we think is the best at that time, never looking down the road at how it can affect those closest to us. Sometimes, never caring how it can affect them. Helen's decision to not tell Eric she was pregnant, was the best decision for her and for him. He was married, with three children and she didn't want the scandal or the headache that could have come with the whole ordeal. So, when he walked away and dropped all contact, she let him. Thinking back, Helen never thought she's ever run into him again. They didn't congregate in the same places or with the same people. For certain, it was never considered that Kamryn would need to know who he was because Helen made sure everything her daughter ever needed was provided for her. And what she couldn't provide, her parents did. Now, with the reality of Eric knowing she exists and Kam working for Michael, it was only a matter of time before Eric let her know who he was. When she asked, during their lunch meet, if he had said anything to Michael about Kam, he said he hadn't, but she could tell that he was lying. She still knew him like the back of her hand. With Michael aware of who Kam really was to him, Helen knew she needed to come clean with Kam before someone else spilled the beans. She didn't know how.

The phone ringing snaps Helen out of her thoughts. "Hello?"

"Hi Mama. What are you doing?" Kamryn says joyfully.

"Just sitting her thinking about you. What are you doing Kam?"

"On my way to rehearsal with the band."

"Well aren't you a busy little something. How are things going there?"

"Yes ma'am, I try to keep busy. After rehearsal, I'm coming back home to get some rest. I'm bartending tonight. I have some exciting news though mama! Guess what?" Kamryn is bursting with excitement to share with her mother the news of the music executives and DJs that Michael gave her yesterday.

"What sweetheart?"

"Michael said that he has scheduled some music people to come hear me sing this weekend. Isn't that wonderful Mama? I can't believe it! I'm so excited that I want to scream. Well, I actually did scream a couple of times already but every time I think about it I want to scream again."

"That is wonderful baby. I'm so happy for you. This is what you've been working for and now it's coming into fruition. You should be excited and scream!"

"Thank you, mama, for your support, your love, and standing by me. I wouldn't be here if it wasn't for you. I can't believe this is happening to me…for me. Michael says that these will be big names in the music business and that he is counting on me to make a wonderful impression. And guess what else he said mama?"

"What else did he say baby?"

"He told me I was his family."

"What do you mean?" Helen suddenly feels herself begin to sweat

"He said, that I'm his family."

"In what way?" Helen asks nervously hoping that he didn't tell Kam that he is her brother.

"In the sense of the bar family ma. I think he just meant that he's looking out for me as family does. What's the matter?"

"Nothing baby. It caught me off guard that he would say something like that to you. That's all."

"Ma, I've told you before, they look at me like a little sister. That should make you feel a little better knowing that more people are looking out for me than Mr. And Mrs. Boozer where I live."

"It does baby. It gives me comfort knowing there are more people looking out for you in that city." Helen tries to clean up her frantic tone. "Now, he says these people are coming this weekend? Are you ready?"

"I'm nervous as heck. But I believe I'm ready. I made sure to give it all I had today at practice. But ma, I really would like it you could be here. I'll feel better knowing this is something I can share with you. You're my best friend.

Please come ma. Please! I know you just left here a few weeks ago, but ma, I need you!"

"I'm scheduled to work this weekend Kam. Let me see if I can get someone to cover my shift or switch with me. I'll do my best to be there baby. But no promises just yet. I'll let you know for sure tomorrow if I can get there." Helen's eyes drop to the floor. She's not scheduled to work this weekend at all. She was hoping that would change Kam's mind. But in true Kam fashion, she wants what she wants. The truth is Helen is trying to avoid coming back to Horns. The last thing she wants to do is run into Eric again. Or even worse, Eric and his wife.

"I understand ma. But you have a few days to make it happen. I'm not trying to pressure you. But having you here would mean everything to me."

"Let me see what I can do Kamryn." Helen says.

"Ok mama. Thank you so much. Alright, I gotta go. I'm walking into rehearsal right now and the band is waiting for me. I love you ma."

"I love you too baby. Talk to you soon." Helen hangs up and sits down in her recliner. Looks like she's going to be back in the city soon. She has never let Kamryn down and she is not going to start now. She made this bed, now she must lay in it. And if laying in it requires telling Kam the truth about her father, then that's what she must do. Now that Eric knows, she can't put it off for long. In her mind, she's encouraging herself to be strong and thinking about how she is going to tell her only child about the decision she made years ago. "Lord, how is my baby going to take this news?' Helen drops to her knees and prays for guidance and counsel.

Chapter Sixteen

Horns is packed tonight, Michael can tell that he is close to capacity. The VIP is almost full, the kitchen is busy, and the bartenders and table servers are moving like lightening. Michael is glad he thought ahead and brought in extra staff. It's a great night and they are expecting an even greater show from our star. Watching the front door, Michael sees Helen waiting to get in and motions for the doorman to let her in, no cover charge. As she enters the main floor, Michael steps up to her and introduces himself.

"Hello Helen. I'm Michael, the owner of Horns. Thank you for coming to see Kamryn perform again. I know she will be ecstatic to see you tonight, especially with it being such a big night for her career. I know there's no one she trusts more than you."

"Thank you, Michael." Helen searches his face for a sign that he really knows who Kamryn is. "And I must thank you for looking out for my little girl while she has been working here. She speaks very highly of you and your staff."

"Kamryn is very special. More special than I could have ever thought or imagined. It has been my pleasure to look after her. It's the least I can do. She is like a little sister to me and what type of brother would I be to not be here for her should she need anything." Michael says with conviction but no bitterness.

"Thank you." Helen says.

"Let me show you to your seat." He offers his arm and leads Helen to the VIP section where he has saved a section for her to watch the show without people walking in front of her. "Enjoy yourself. Whatever you want is on the house. Thank you for everything. Kamryn will always be welcome and safe here. I hope that you believe that."

"I do Michael." She pats his hand and takes a seat. "Thank you again."

Michael walks away and he's sure his implied comments hit home just as he had planned for them to. He only wanted her to know that he was aware of who Kamryn was and that he had her back always. Back on the main floor, he walks around and greats the customers. He had invited Lena, Evan, and Evan's girlfriend to the show as well. He was holding two booths in VIP for them as well. Word had been left at the door to let them in directly, past the line. The show was scheduled to start in half an hour. He wanted his brother to see Kamryn perform before he tells him who she really is. His father asked him not to tell anyone but just like his father, Evan was his best friend too and to keep this from him was unfair.

Lost in his thoughts, he doesn't hear anyone come up behind him until they touch his shoulder. Turning around, he stares into the eyes of Lena. She looks amazingly sexy and tasty tonight.

"Damn woman, what you tryin to do dressed like that? You look good as fuck. You bouta make me take you in my office and bless my desk with that fat ass."

"Cut it out Michael. But thank you, all the same." Lena does a little spin to allow him to get the full effect of her yellow top and black liquid pants.

"That ass is sitting up right too. I'm gonna may have to fuck somebody up in here tonight for lookin at you too hard. Let me take your ass up to this VIP so you can sit down."

"You're a mess." Lena says and laughs as Michael grabs her hand and leads the way to VIP.

"That's right, your mess. Speaking of being yours, when are we going to go pick out this engagement ring?"

"You want me to pick my own ring? Hell no. You can take me to get sized, but you're picking out the ring you think I deserve."

"Alright Boo. I can do that. We'll go tomorrow. I mean, you already said yes. The ring is just for show."

"Speaking of a show. You asked me to come see this young lady sing. Is she that good?"

"She's amazing. I asked you to come, so we could hang out. But I also want you to think about taking her on a client. Shit this club, I know like the back of my hand. But what will come for her in the music business, I have no idea. Remember I told you I invited some producers and DJs to the club to hear her sing? Well, some of them are here tonight. They're sitting in VIP with you at the other tables. I don't want them talking to her without someone who knows the business being right there with her best interest at heart."

"Why are you going through all of this for someone you just met? Is it because she works for you?"

"Naw babe," he leans in closer to her ear. "she's my sister. Long story that we can get into later. But I need her to be protected."

"Oh, shit. Alright baby, I got you, you know that."

"Thank you love." Michael kisses her cheek. "I have to head back down to the main floor. I'm waiting on my brother and his girl to get here. I also have a feeling my Pop is going to show up. And I don't want no static. Kamryn's mother is sitting in the booth over there. If my Pop sees her, it might get a little ugly and I don't want that to happen."

"Ok baby. Hurry back up when you can."

"You think I'm about to leave you sitting here alone all night, looking like this? You must be fuckin crazy. I'll be back as soon as the show starts. I hired a comedienne to MC the show all weekend. Wanted to give the patrons something new. Change it up a little bit." He kisses Lena on the lips and touches his fingers to her chin. "Love you."

"Love you too." Lena says in return and picks up the tablet to place her drink and food order. "Out of the corner of her eye, she sees the woman Michael pointed out as Kamryn's mother looking her way. "She's gorgeous." Lena says to herself.

Now standing by the bar, Michael notices his brother enter Horns, with his girlfriend in tow. Michael waves his hand, motioning for his brother to come to the bar. They embrace immediately as they do every time they see each other.

"Mike, what's up? Thanks for the invite."

"Come on bruh. When have you ever needed an invite to come here? The last time you came, you didn't give me the courtesy of saying hello or nothing. Just in and out after the show, you even paid the cover. What was all that about?"

"Awe damn, Mike. Why you doin me like that in front of my lady?" He motions to Miracle. "Miracle, this is my brother Michael. He owns this beautiful place and has always been my guardian since the day I was born."

"Hello Michael."

"What's up Miracle. My brother was right, you are gorgeous." He watches as she blushes. "Leek, damn, bruh. You did good."

"Thanks Mike, yeah, I'm damn sure the lucky one in this relationship."

"I saved you a table in VIP. Before I take you up, I want to wrap with you for a minute. Is that alright Miracle?" Michael looks at Miracle for confirmation.

"Absolutely."

"Thank you beautiful. Yo, CT, give this lady whatever she wants, on the house."

"You got it boss. What can I get you miss?"

Michael and Maleek walk to his office and close the door. "What's up bruh? You alright?"

"Yeah, I'm cool Leek. Two things I want to let you know. One, Lena is here and she's up in VIP already. She's in the booth next to yours. And two, I asked her to marry me and she said yes."

"Get the fuck outta here! Are you serious right now?"

"Dead ass serious bruh. I love her and I asked her a few weeks ago. She said yes. Now I still have to take her to meet mama. That's the issue!"

"Damn Mike. Yeah that is going to be an issue. Mama hasn't met her and you asked for her hand in marriage? You must be pussy whipped dude."

"Naw, it's not like that. Well shit, maybe it is a little bit. But I still love her, even if mama doesn't like her. I'm still gonna marry her."

"I hear you and you know I got your back, but damn, can I at least meet her and shit before you walk down the aisle?" They both fall out laughing.

"I'm going to introduce you as soon as I take you up. Don't mention the engagement though. I'm bringing her to Mama's July fourth party and getting down on one knee and everything. No matter what!"

"Ok. I'm with you Mike. Now, can I get back to my woman. I know those clowns out there are lickin their chops tryin to see if she alone."

"That's why I left CT to watch over her. Ain't nobody walkin up on her with him right there. That dude is a monster and more protective than a pitbull who just had pups."

"That's all good but that's my woman and I'm not takin any chances."

"I can dig it. I wouldn't either. Shit, I rushed Lena up to VIP when she got here." They laugh together at their comments.

"Alright Mike, come on and introduce me to your woman. As much as you've talked about her, I feel like I already know her but a real introduction would be great. Especially since it sounds like she's going to be my sister in law."

"For sho."

They leave the office and meet Miracle back at the bar where they left here. CT walks away when they approach and they head over to the VIP section. They walk up to the booth where Lena and sitting sipping on her drink.

"Lena. Baby, this is my lil brother Maleek and his girlfriend Miracle. Leek and Miracle, this is my lady Lena." Hello's are said and Maleek and Miracle sit down in the booth next to Lena. Michael walks over and sits on her other side. Small talk begins and after fifteen minutes, Michael again excuses himself to walk through the club again before the show begins.

"Looks good in here son."

"Pop. I knew you were comin tonight." Michael hugs his father.

"Yeah. I want to see how she does. Did any of those music producers show up?"

"Yeah, they're up in VIP already. Lena, Maleek, and his girl are up there too."

Eric looks up at and instantly sees Helen. "So, is Helen huh?"

"Pop, don't start nothin with her ok. This is a big weekend for Kamryn and I want her to have the positive attention she deserves."

"I'm not son. Tonight, is not about me and Helen, it's about Kamryn.

Besides, I already told Helen what I thought and what I want. It's on her to do it right now. Am I sitting with you guys or did you get me my own booth?"

"You can chill with us. It'll give you a chance to meet the ladies and talk to them. I was thinking maybe we go get something to eat after the show."

"Sounds like a plan and looks like the show is about to start. Let's go so we don't miss anything."

Outside, all Gavin hears are people talking about the young singer they're waiting in line to hear. And it's all the things he loves to hear, especially about a new artist that he's scoping. When Michael called asking him to come through, he thought maybe it was one of those things where Mike was smashing the wanna be star and made promises that he had to keep. With that in mind, Gavin almost changed his mind and went to another spot tonight. But once the car pulled up to Horns and he peeped line, Gavin shook his head in approval and knew he'd made the right decision to keep his word and roll through. Knowing his name is already on the list to bypass the line, Gavin approaches the doorman.

"What's up Bruh? Gavin Ellis from Vysin Records."

Sam checks the list for Gavin's name and crosses it out. "Come right in Mr. Ellis. Michael is probably up in the VIP already. I believe he has a booth reserved for you as well. I'll let him know you're here." Sam steps aside allowing Gavin room to pass through.

"Thanks, Bruh. All these people are here to see Kamryn?"

"Yes sir." Sam smiled.

"Is it always like this? I mean is the crowd always this deep for one unknown singer?"

"Every weekend. She's fire son!"

"Damn! I'm gonna make hit up the bar. Can you let Mike know he can find there?"

"I'll let him know. Enjoy the show." Sam raises his left wrist to speak into the small microphone hidden in his sleeve to notify the security team and Michael of Gavin's arrival.

Gavin steps into the building and views the crowd. "Damn, this place is packed," he says to himself. "How good is this girl?"

Making his way through the crowd, Gavin notices how everyone is vibing to the band and enjoying themselves. At the bar, he orders a drink then turns to look around again. He remembers the first time he came through Horns after it had opened. It had a small crowd back then but nothing compared to tonight. He can see why Mike expanded and added the two VIP sections. Horns has become a money maker for his fraternity brother and from the looks of it, he must be making money hand over fist now.

"Gav! Glad you made it bruh!" Michael shouts a little to be heard over the music.

"Mike, what's up bruh? Thanks for the invite!" The men embrace in their normal brotherly way smiling.

"Shit, you know you never need an invite to come through here."

"Yeah, I know. I just don't get through this city as much as I used to."

"Well, being a big record executive, I'm sure you're busy bruh. I'm just glad you were going to be in town this weekend for the awards show and could come through. It means a lot man. Let's go over to VIP, I want you to meet my lady. Did you order a drink already?"

"Yeah, I'm just waitin on your man to bring it back so I can pay for it." Just as he finished his statement, Block brings the drink back.

"Yo, Block, his drinks are on me. Add it to my tab from VIP."

"You got it boss."

"Bruh, that's not necessary. Let me pay for my shit. I ain't come here for nothing free."

"Naw bruh, that's not how this shit goes. You're here as a guest of mine. You don't pay for shit." Michael turns and Gavin follows him as they walk over to the VIP section. Once up the short flight of stairs, they walk side by side to their booth.

"Baby, this is my frat brother, Gavin Ellis. Gavin, this is my fiancée, Lena." Lena stands to greet Gavin.

"Damn bruh, your fiancée? That's something I never thought I'd hear you say. Wonderful to meet you Lena. I know to get my boy here to settle down, you have to be one hell of a woman." He steps in to give hug her.

"Well, I'll agree with you on the part that I'm one hell of a woman." Lena laughs. "It's just as wonderful to meet you too Gavin. Michael has told me so much about you and your college years and adventures." She laughs again.

"Yeah, well don't believe half of them. And the rest are probably true but embellished. Maleek, what's up with you?" Gavin says as he reaches over to give Maleek a brotherly hug.

"Oh, I can't call it Gav. It's good to see you though! Babe, this is Gavin Ellis. Gav, this is my lady, Miracle."

"Nice to meet you Miracle."

"Nice to meet you as well Gavin." Miracle smiles.

"Gav, what brings you into the city? You here for the awards tomorrow?" Maleek asks.

"Yeah man. Plus, Mike called and invited me. Thought I'd come and bless the spot with my presence."

"No doubt! I'm guessing he invited you to listen to Kamryn?"

"Yeah, he told me the young lady is exceptional in her style and vocal skills. I thought I'd come through and kill two birds with one stone. Listen to some good music and see my bruhs. And from the looks of everything, he must not have been lying because this joint is packed to the rim and the line outside is ridiculous."

"Bruh, her vocals are amazing. Miracle and I came through last month and she blew us away with her performance."

"Well that's why I'm here. I wanna see if she could be someone I can get on the label. If she's as good as you say, then I'm very interested to see what she can do."

"Well, we'll let you make your own mind up about her skills." Michael says. The lights dim a little as the spotlight on the stage shines on the single microphone stand. "The show's about to start."

"Good evening Horns! For those of you who don't know, I'm Eye

Holla and I'll be your MC for the night! Thank you all for coming out! Now, I know you're wondering how did I get this gig right? Normally, you are all greeted by the handsome Michael Dane and all the ladies get to tap the woman next to them and say, "Girl, you see this nigga? Damn! Damn! Damn! He is finer than a bitch hair after a silk press!" The crowd laughs. "But not tonight! Tonight, you get me. This whole weekend, you get me! So, if you plan on coming back out tomorrow, you'll see my ass right back up here again. But maybe, I'll wear my afro wig instead of this 22-inch human hair! You know a sista gotta stay fly always. And I gotta keep you all guessin and askin yourselves, 'What is this bitch gone look like next?' Long as I don't come out lookin like Madea, I should be straight." The crowd laughs again.

"For those of you looking for Michael, he's here. He just decided to chill for the night instead of being up here entertaining y'all. Which works for me, because I could use the check!" Laughter again. Eye Holla continues to tell more jokes and comical references for another fifteen minutes.

"Alright, I think I've stalled enough and I know y'all came here tonight to see the beautiful Kamryn and listen to the sounds of the amazing Soulful Sounds." The crowd whistles and cheers as Eye Holla introduces the band members. "Now without any additional hesitation, give a hug round of applause for the incredible Kamryn!" The crowd stands to their feet as Kamryn walks onto the stage and hugs Eye Holla.

Stepping up to the microphone, the crowd takes their seats and the room quiets to hear her. "Good evening everyone. Every night I come out here to sing, I am so honored and flattered to see you all sitting out there. I always hoped but never in my wildest dreams could have imagined the love I've received from you all. This has been the most unbelievable experience of my life." The crowd erupts with applause and some people even stand-up.

"She's so humble." Gavin says to Michael.

"I know, right. She is one of a kind bruh." They both turn their heads back towards the stage.

"I wanted to say thank you to Michael Dane for giving the opportunity to get up here on this stage and do what I love to do the most. It means everything to me that he believes in me." Again, applause as the spotlight finds Michael in VIP and he stands to wave hello. "I think my Mom is here tonight too. Mom, where are you?" Helen stands up from the VIP area and a spotlight finds her. The sounds from the audience get louder to show their appreciation for her. "Without that woman, I don't know where I'd be in life. She has always been my biggest cheerleader and greatest fan. My Mom is everything to me."

Helen blows Kamryn a kiss and sits back down. Eric watches the exchange and feels the twinge of jealousy wanting to be included in Kamryn's words of love and admiration. A tear forms in his eye but he wipes it away before it can fall then looks around to see if anyone is watching him. He looks right into the eyes of Michael, who smiles at his father. Eric shakes his head slightly to confirm he's ok.

"As I prepared for tonight's performance, I went through several song selections in my head. I was trying to figure out what I wanted to sing about and if I wanted it to be a sort of melody reflecting my appreciation and love for the support you have all shown. Or did I want to put you in the mood of loving each other by listening to my words and then gazing at your partners with lust or with love? Did I want to make you want to run out of here so you could be alone or have you in your seats until my voice ended? And what I came up with is a selection of songs that are special to me. Lyrics and pieces that express my love for music and I hope you all will see my love through the words." She looks into the eyes of those in the front row and smiles.

"Tonight, I'm going to start with a song I wrote with our own house band, Soulful Sounds. It's a piece we've been working on for some time and we have agreed that here is no better time than tonight to let you all hear it and be the judge. It's not perfect but we wanted to share it with you." The music starts to play in the background softly. "And when it's done, you let us know what you think about it, ok? Can y'all do that for us Horns?" Voices raise in the building confirming their agreeance with multitudes of "yes," "ok," and "we got you baby girl" as the volume from the band grows louder like she had just turned up the speakers.

"At night, I used to dream of you. Wondering are you dreamin of me too? Pieces of me missin when I would learn somethin new. There was a time, when I didn't know where I'd be, who I was, would I ever see. The truth that was my heart, my life, my pride. In my darkest times, you stepped in and found. The life I had still inside, the force that was my sound. You opened my eyes to see things clear. Allowed me to speak with hesitation, no fear. You opened my ears to hear, it was there all along, what I thought was missin. The voice inside, but I wasn't listenin. Thank you, music for being my shield, my cover, my shelter. You saved me from myself when there was no other. You are the voice in the dark, cryin out to me. You are the love in my heart, that's set me free. You are the spirit in the air, the wind beneath my wings. Now watch me soar with the pleasure it brings. When it's all said and done, I will be free. To be the me I've always wanted to be. No more tears to cry, or battles to fight. Only joy on the other side no matter day or night." The music plays as everyone grooves to smooth sounds of the bank and the hypnotic sound of Kamryn's voice. With her eyes closed and a smile on her face, she revels in the words that she has written as she shares them with the place that gave her the courage to go after her dreams.

Helen watches emotionally as she is overcome with joy for her daughter. The pride she feels for her daughter is evident to anyone who is watching her and Eric was doing just that. He wanted so much to get up from his seat and go over and sit next to her as their daughter sang to them all. He can't remember ever wanting anything else as much. Watching Kamryn from his seat he feels overwhelmed with his own emotions and the only person who knows even an ounce of what he's feeling, is the mother of his only daughter. But he knows that he can't approach her for more reasons than one.

Michael holds Lena's hand and leans into her, pressing his chest into her back. Lena responds instantly, leaning back into her man. Miracle turns to look in the eyes of Maleek and he tilts his head to stare into hers. He leans forward to place a kiss on her lips. The entire room is filled with the essence of

91

love and emotions as Kamryn sings and the band plays. All eyes are on the stage watching as the melody of the song can be heard by the crowd outside still waiting to get in.

Helen looks down into the main seating area at the audience who is now entirely captivated by her daughter's voice and words. She turns to look through the VIP sections and looking far right, she sees Eric watching Kamryn. And as if he can feel her stares, he turns to look at back at her in return. A smile spreads across his face to show his own pride in the daughter he never knew that she raised alone. Even in the dark, she can see his entire face. He mouthed the words "thank you" to her for being the backbone and sole supporter of a child he never knew he had but was already so fond of. Helen mouthed "you're welcome" to him and turned back to watch their daughter.

Kamryn sings the last note of the song and looks directly at her mother and says, "I love you Mama." With the last notes of the music playing the room is quiet. Kamryn looks at the faces of those looking back at her and holds her breath. All at once, the room is on its feet cheering and applauding for her original words and the bands beautiful delivery of its companied notes. Kamryn exhales the breath of full relief and bows in response to the praise.

"What did I tell you Gav? She's amazing right?"

"Yo son, she's ready. I'm gonna stay for the whole set, but I want to schedule a meeting with her tomorrow. Tonight, is her night and let her enjoy it. Does she have an agent?"

"Yeah. Lena is going to be her agent. I'll make sure they both ae at the meeting. Since you're staying the whole set, we can discuss a meeting time after closing in my office."

"Bet." Gavin shakes his head and they turn back to the stage to finish watching the show.

Chapter Seventeen

"Eric?" Zyera walks into Eric's home office to talk to him.

"Yes dear." Eric looks up from what he's writing to see Zyera walking towards him. He smiles at his wife. "Woman, I swear you look more beautiful every day I'm married to you."

"I know," she giggles. "Look how lucky you are to have a wife like me."

"You don't know the half of it."

"Everything is ready for fourth. I hired Touch of Class Party Planning to transform the backyard and pool. They always do such a beautiful job. And I ordered the cake from SweetsByShiffawn and those amazing candy mangos from All You Can Sweet. Is there anything specific that you want besides that?"

"No love, that should be fine. What about the fireworks?"

"Williams Fireworks will be providing the show for the children and our guests. They are sending someone to the party."

"Good, I didn't want to mess with those things this year. I'm getting too old for that shit."

"If my memory serves me correctly, the boys took care of the fireworks last year." She laughs and walks around his desk to sit on it in front of him.

"I don't remember that part." He looks up at her from his chair and puts his hand on her thigh.

She covers it with her own. "Yes, you wouldn't."

"Love, I wanted to invite some other people to the party if that's alright with you."

"Of course, honey. You can invite anyone you want. It is someone from work? The grands always love when you invite celebrities to things."

"No, it's not a celebrity." He says and looks down.

"Alright. The more the merrier. I'm so happy all the children will be here."

"Thank you love. So am I." Eric says.

"I talked to Evan and Edward called yesterday and told me they will be bringing dates as well. Sounds like we're going to have a full house. I'm excited to meet these women. I hope this new one Evan is dating is not like that last hussy. She was not what I envisioned for my son and she wasn't good enough for him. I knew she only wanted his money and that she didn't love my baby. And I knew it was only a matter of time until he found out. When he did, I swear I wanted to through a party because he was done with her."

"Zyera, you can't control who these boys date. You must let them live and find their own happiness. Just like I found you, they will find the ones for them."

"Don't tell me what I can do with my boys. I'm not letting anyone use them. I want them to find love and have a family. I'm ready for more grandchildren. Hopefully grandchildren that live closer than Eric and his family."

"I know love." He pats her thigh before placing it back on his desk.

"Alright then." Zyera stands next to her husband. "What are you writing?" She looks down at the paper on Eric's desk.

"Nothing much. Just my thoughts. Nothing for you to be concerned about." His hand slightly covers the paper.

"Alright then. I'll leave you to it." She bends to kiss the top of his head. "Love you."

"I love you too." He watches her walk out of the office. Once she's gone, he looks down at the paper on his desk to read the words he had written moments before she'd interrupted his thoughts. The words on the page were not just any letter, but a letter he was writing for Kamryn. A letter he planned to give to her to tell her all about him and her brothers. A letter that would explain his side of the story and why he had been absent in her life all these years. But was he going to be able to give it to her? Helen told him she would tell Kamryn who he was but he had no idea if she had kept her word. Kamryn still hasn't reached out to him or said anything to Michael about knowing who they were to each other.

"Yo, Pop! Where are you?"

"I'm in my office Mike." Michael walks into his father's office and closes the door. At the desk, he gives Eric a hug and then sits in one of the chairs opposite his father. "What you doin?"

"Honestly? Trying to write a letter to Kamryn to tell her who I am. It's the only thing I can think of right now. I want to get to know her and her to know me. I've missed the first twenty-one years. I don't want to miss anymore. I've been thinking of inviting her and Helen to the fourth of July party your mother is throwing. Get it all out in the open."

"Pop, I don't know if that's a good idea. You know how Ma is and if you just spring all of this on her like that, who knows how she will react. And if I know Mom, she's invited a lot of people here. Are you certain that will be the right place and time to tell her and them?"

"Son, I have to face this head on and let the chips fall where they may. I don't want to live another year without my daughter. Your mother is strong. I just hope and pray she will forgive me for this."

"Look Pop. I don't know what Ma will do. But I do know that she will be hurt and possibly embarrassed. This just sounds like a conversation you need to have with her alone. Not with a house full of people. I'm just sayin, think about this. If you want, I'll invite Kamryn and her mother to the party. That may take a little bit of pressure off you, but you gotta tell Ma. Tell her before that girl and her mother step one foot inside this house. Otherwise, Ma may never forgive you. I know you think that this will be the best time to introduce her, especially with Eric being in town but put your own feelings to the side and think of Ma and Kam before your own feelings. They both deserve to know the whole story."

"When the fuck did you get so smart?"

"I guess I get it from my Pop!" They both laugh. "Did Ma tell you I'm bringin a date?"

"She told me today. You bringing Lena?"

"Who else? Pop, I asked her to marry me and she said yes. I haven't given her a ring yet though. I wanted to officially do it at the party, surrounded by family."

"Wow son. Congratulations! That's big!"

"Yeah man. It's time and she is the one. Pop, she's the one."

"I'm happy for you. I like her too. I haven't told your mother I met her already though. You know how she is."

"Yeah, I get it. I hope Ma likes her."

"When she sees how happy you are, she will be fine. Your mother has always wanted what was best for you guys. Remember how she was when she first me Eric Jr's wife? She was on that poor girl like Interstate 95 on a holiday weekend. Drilled that poor girl with question after question for what seemed like hours. Now, she loves her like she birthed her."

"I remember. We were all worried about her that day. She held strong though and once Ma realized how much she loved Jr. Ma was fine. I'm not worried about Lena though. She's the strongest woman I know, next to Ma. They share some of the same qualities to be quite honest. That's what drew me to her from the start. The first day I met her, she wasn't taking none of my shit or fallin for the lines that I normally gave to women. She walked away from me a few times and kept me real distant. I had to work for her harder than I had to work for any woman in my life which made me want her even more."

"Those are the ones you keep son. Those women are hard to come by these days and when you find one, it's in your best interest to lock her down."

"That's the plan Pop. That's the plan. I'm going to see the jeweler today to order her engagement ring. Maleek's meeting me there at four." He checks his watch. "I need to get going now as a matter of fact." Standing, he looks at his father. "Pop, think about what I said. The party is next week. Don't spring this news on Ma like that. You gotta talk to her first."

"I know son. Before you go, how did things go with Gavin and Kamryn? Is he going to sign her?"

"We had a premeeting and thankfully Lena is going to represent her so she can look out for her. It looks like something good is going to happen for Kam. She was excited when we met with him. Gavin had her do a studio session to record the song she sang at her show the night he was there. Said he's taking that back to the record company for them to listen to it and get their reviews. But its lookin good."

"Wonderful. If she needs anything, let me know. I'll pay for it."

"Alright Pop." He smiles and walks over to the door to leave. He puts his hand on the knob then turns slightly to look back at his father. "Pop?"

"Yes?"

"I just wanted you to know that I don't think any less of you for what happened years ago. The affair with Helen and then finding out after twenty years, you share a daughter with her, that's tough. I know you've been beating yourself up about it too. Once you tell Ma, you'll feel some of that pain lifted off your shoulders. But you gotta tell her. It's the right thing to do. Especially if you are tryin to be in Kam's life. Just remember, you can't force that either. For as long as I can remember, you have been a great father and provider for all of us. Nothing can take that away from you, nor has it changed how I see you now. As a man, we have all made decisions and choices we regret. I'm not saying you regret Kam, I'm saying that things happen and all we can do is deal with them the best way we know how. Even though this is unexpected, I'm happy to have a little sister and I'm sure my brothers will feel the same way. And I'm proud of you for wanting to do what you can for Kam now."

Eric rises from the desk and walks over to his son. "Thank you, Mike. I will talk to your mother and your brothers about this. I want them to hear it from me and I will tell them before the party. You have my word."

"Alright Pop. I gotta go, I'll holla at you later." Michael opens the door to see his mother standing on the other side with tears running down her cheeks and her mouth slightly ajar. The look in Zyera's eyes says more than any words could ever express. Michael looks at her and then back to his father. Eric drops his head and closes his eyes.

Finally looking up, he says, "Thank you, son. You better get going. I need to talk to your mother."

"Love you Pop." He turns to his mother. "I love you Ma." He pulls her in for a hug and whispers in her ear, "I don't know if you heard everything, but please Ma, give him a chance to explain. Please, for me." He steps back and looks into her eyes. He can read the pain she is feeling. "Please Ma."

Zyera looks into the eyes of her middle son, "Love you sweetheart." She says as she turns around and walks up the stairs towards the bedroom she shares with Eric.

Michael looks back at his father and winks. Then steps around his mother and leaves his parents standing there looking at each other. Each showing their own pain. "Good luck Pop." He whispers as he reaches the front door.

Eric stands in the hallway outside of his office and watches his wife of more than three decades walk away from him. Now, he must face the music of the song he wrote years ago. In his head, he thinks of a way to start his confession. "The facts are the facts. There is really nothing I can do to change them or alter the reality of this situation. This is the time and we're at the point where the only thing I can do is be honest and offer to you my confession on what is going on. I didn't know how I was going to tell you or even how I was going to find the nerve to bring this to you. The only thing I could think of was to do it this way." Eric paces in his office and stops to look in the mirror. "Hell naw. That shit is not going to work. She's gonna kill my ass." For weeks he's been trying to figure out how to tell Zyera about Kamryn, Helen, and the events that took place over twenty years ago and now he has no choice but to put it on the table here and now.

"Fuck it! I'll just say it how it comes out." He tells himself and follows the path Zyera just walked. He finds her in their bedroom just as he had thought, sitting on the chaise.

"Hello my love. We should talk." He bends to kiss her before settling next to her on the chaise.

"Ok." Zyera marks her book before closing it and setting it to the side.

As Eric gets comfortable, she leans into her him and he allows him to place an arm around her pulling her in close.

"Before I begin, I'm going to ask something of you first." He looks down at the top of her head. "I know you heard some of what Mike and I were saying downstairs. But can you give me a chance to speak it through before you say anything?"

She tries to pull away a little to look in his eyes but he holds her tighter keeping her in place. "I will give you a chance to say what you need to say."

"Thank you, my love." Eric takes a deep breath and exhales slowly.

"You know that you are the most important person in my life. Nothing I've ever done will ever overshadow or surpass the love I have for you. You are my backbone, my queen, my strength and my weakness all in one. I would lay down my life to save yours without a second thought. The day you walked into my life, I became a completed man. You have helped me grow and build this life that we have. You are the reason why I am, the man that I am today. I know that I am the luckiest man alive to have you in my life, as my partner, as my love, my wife, my best friend, and the other half of my soul. I knew it the first day I met you that you would be my wife." He takes a deep breath and the continues with a quivering voice. "But there was a time when I was lost. Twenty years ago, I was lost within myself; lost within our marriage; lost within my own head. I never doubted my love for you. I never doubted your love for me. I was teaching during this time and allowed myself to be weak and broke the vows I promised never to break as we stood in front of the preacher. I made the decision to step out on you, on our marriage, on our family." Formed tears begin to fall down his face as he breaths become shallow. But being a woman of her word, Zyera sits still and quiet in his arms as he continues to speak. "My irresponsible behavior left the door open for another to step in and give me what I thought I was missing. What I thought I was looking for. What I thought I didn't already have."

"For a year, I carried on this affair with a woman that was in one of my lecture classes while you were home with the boys being a wife and a mother.

Then one day, you walked into my classroom during a lecture. And not just any class. You walked into the class where this woman was sitting. I heard the door open and looked over into your face and then I looked at hers. When I looked back at you, you smiled and took a seat. And my heart broke. Not because I thought I was caught but because it became so real to me what I had been doing to you without you even knowing. That day, I walked away from that woman and never looked back. Never spoke to her again. Never contacted her again." Eric looks down again at the head of his wife as she lays on his chest quiet. "I never looked at another woman in that manner after that day. The thought never crossed my mind again to step outside of our marriage. From that day forward, I've dedicated myself to making sure our marriage was what it was meant to be. That I gave every ounce of love and affection and attention to you and our boys. Every game, concert, awards ceremony, and graduation, I made sure I was there to support them and most of all you."

"For the past twenty years, I never thought about that woman once. Slightly because of fear that you could read my mind. But more importantly because I knew that if you found out, the pain it would cause could ruin our lives together. Could end our marriage. Maybe even damage our boys." Eric takes another deep breath and prepares to tell her the final piece of this sorted puzzle.

"A few months ago, I went to Horns to see how the club was doing and hear the singer Mike has been telling us about. While I was there, I looked through the crowd and I saw her. The woman from twenty years ago, was sitting in Horns. At first, I thought it was a dream or a nightmare really. I thought to myself, how could this be? I went over to see if I was dreaming or if it was truly her and it was. I asked her what she was doing there? She told me she was at Horns to hear her daughter sing. Her daughter came on stage and when I looked at her, I commented on how beautiful she was. And the woman," he pauses to find the courage to finish his statement. "the woman tells me, that her daughter is also my daughter." He stops and holds his breath. Sensing he still has more to say, Zyera pats his abdomen. Eric exhales. "She tells me that the young woman on stage singing, is my daughter. Her name is Kamryn. When I asked her why she never told me about Kamryn, she said it was because she didn't want to ruin my marriage. She told me that she knew the affair was just an affair of the body, not of the heart. The woman never told Kamryn about me or who I truly am. She raised her with the help of her parents." The tears are flowing down Eric's face freely as he continues to talk to his wife.

"I'm sorry love. I'm sorry that I put you in this position to deal with. I'm sorry that I was weak as fuck and allowed this to happen. I'm sorry about it all. I don't want you to leave me and if you decide that's what you want to do, I'll fight you to stay and I'll do whatever I have to do so you will. But the one thing I gotta be honest about, is I want to know her. I want to know Kamryn. I want to know my daughter. I want her to know her brothers. I want her to know you. I'm sorry if that hurts you to hear love. I'm sorry. And if you don't want her here in our home, then I'll do it away from you. But I want you to know that I've already missed the first twenty years of her life and I don't want to miss anymore. I don't want to hide this from you." Sobs escape his body as he holds Zyera tighter than he's ever held her. The fear that she will get up and leave overwhelms Eric to the edge of what feels like his world.

Zyera allows her husband to cry and hold her for as long as he needs to until his sobs quiet and his breathing returns to normal. Never raising her head to check on him or see if he's finished, she rubs her hand across his chest to soothe him as she would do their sons when they were babies and fussing. Taking her own deep breath, she speaks to him softly. "This woman, her name is Helen. Before I walked in that day, I watched you from the small window in the door. I watched you give your lecture and the interactions you had with your students. I saw you look at her several times as she sat in the front row. I watched her eyes sparkle as she marveled in your brilliance. And I saw her face when I walked in. I knew what the look was. It wasn't of shock or horror. It wasn't the look of betrayal. It was the look of a woman who had come face to face with reality. Not seeing me but knowing is different than seeing me and knowing. After I walked into your lecture that day, she stared at me until the end of class. That's when I knew who she was. That's when there was no doubt in my mind and my heart what you had been doing for the past year." Zyera snuggles into her husband more. At this point, you can't tell him from her as they look like one body.

"Helen is strong, intelligent, educated, and currently an ICU Nurse Manager. She is very beautiful, still today. Maybe even more beautiful than she was all those years ago. I saw then and I can see now how you could get mesmerized by her. She moved away from the city soon after she found out she was pregnant with Kamryn. And she raised her in a loving and protected home. But she never married. That always made me wonder why. I used to think it was because she was in love with you and that no one measured up to what you shared with each other. Then I came to realize that she was so engulfed in her love for Kamryn that she put her wants and needs aside. She wasn't a nun, she dated throughout the years but never anything too serious and she never brought the men she dated around Kamryn when she was growing up. She wanted to make sure that Kamryn had the best life she could have even without the presence of her father in her life." Eric sits in silence, never releasing his grasp on his wife. Zyera's hand that was sitting on Eric's chest, finds his hand and intertwines hers with his.

"Kamryn has grown into a beautiful woman. When she was little, she had your eyes, but they changed around the time she was two or three. But she's always had your Mother's face. Your Mother's whit. And your Father's charm. I don't know where that voice came from though. She's been singing like that since she was maybe five. Belting out songs that no one knew she could sing or learn. For years, she looked so much like Eric Jr, it shocked me. Then I thought to myself, she is Eric's child and his genes are so strong, she should look like my boys. She won her school spelling bee in the fifth grade. Her word was 'ostentatious'. And she spelled it without missing a beat and looking at Helen the entire time. I was very proud of her for myself and in your absence. In middle school, she got her first heartbreak and was sad for about two months. Helen took her to get ice cream and they went to the park to swing and laugh.

She sang at her high school graduation and it brought tears to the eyes of everyone in the auditorium. Helen cried the entire ceremony. She was accepted into ten colleges but decided she wanted to fulfill her own dreams and live her own life. That's how she ended up back in the city. That young woman has made her mother so proud." Zyera exhales as if a weight has been lifted off her chest. The room is quiet for some time as they lay in each other's arms clinging to each other. Neither speaking, only breathing. Zyera releases her hand from his and pats his chest again. Eric releases his hold on her slowly.

Before raising herself from the chaise, she finally looks at the face of her husband and he sees the tears from her eyes as they roll down her face. Zyera turns and walks into her closet. After a minute, she returns to the chaise with an envelope and a photo album. "I have been waiting for years to give this to you. I found this envelope years ago. It was addressed to me. The photo album I created for you." She sits back in the space she vacated a few minutes earlier.

Eric accepts the envelope and opens it to reveal something he thought he'd thrown out years ago. He remembers this like he wrote it yesterday. His eyes follow the handwritten note as he reads it silently.

"Zyera, I'd call you by my term of endearment but, I assume by now we're on different terms and I'm probably closer to the hate part of your soul. I'm concerned with the failure in the vows that I vowed to love you with. My heart rate has been failing ever since. Nowadays I'm just thankful for these Oxycontin, it controls my analgesia. I'm campaigning for the rain, running an empty race with no supporters. I need to change my pin number. I apologize, but it seems like for seasons I've been stuck in the nature of autumn. Feasting off recalled yeast that made my nature rise solemnly. Here I sit, offering split confessions to the pastor. Lamenting about the past with the pass mistress who was skilled in her profession. I'm drowning in the pasture of gluttony. Feeling like the rapture has rightfully come and I was left. I've been sending you hallmark cards, have you received them? Since then, I've marked hallways with tears from the same ducts that once celebrated you. But, you're still ignoring

them out of ignorance. I'm pouring my heart out to you. But I guess I'm still half empty. I'm pleasantly pleading my case. Please tell me I have an appeal left. With all the love I have to give, I can only hope and trust you can find it in your heart to forgive my indiscretion and violation of your trust. Eric"

"I remember when you would write me poetry every time we had a fight in the beginning. It took me years to understand your style but once I did, I could read between the lines to get to the meaning of your beautiful words. Instead of just buying a card or writing 'I'm sorry,' you would bring me a once cryptic poem that I would have to decipher. I found this in the trash and initially thought it was for Helen. Then after reading it a few times, I knew it was for me and you were saying you were sorry. Even though I did not have an affair, I knew that I was not doing all that I was supposed to be doing as your wife at that time. You were away from us. The boys were little and although we were not struggling financially, we were struggling emotionally between us. I don't think either of us realized the toll being away from each other would take. Only seeing you on the weekends when you could make it home and being gone months on end. That was tough for me, for the boys, and when I found that letter, I finally saw how tough it was on you. When you came home after that last semester of teaching, I saw the change in you. You were so dedicated to us, to our family. I had to know what happened that year you were away. That's when I hired someone to get me more information on Helen. Who she was, where she came from, and whatever else they could dig up. After a few weeks, the investigator came back and told me that Helen was pregnant. I waited for months to see if she would try to contact you or even me to say something. But she never did. I thought she would come to you for help with the child but she didn't. I thought to myself, how strong is this woman? Even after she had an affair with my husband, fully aware that he was a married man, I found myself having a lot of respect for her. That's when I made the choice to keep up with her and Kamryn. I've had some help over the years though with dates of events Kamryn was involved in or attending. I tried to make sure that I was there for you when you couldn't be there for her. I'm not saying I'm ok with the fact that you cheated on me. What I am saying is that you have been a wonderful father to our boys and I know that you would have been a wonderful father to Kamryn if you had known."

"Why didn't you tell me?"

"It wasn't my secret to tell. It's not that I was trying to keep it from you love. I had to respect the fact that Helen had made her decision as the child's mother. If I was in the same shoes, I would've wanted the same thing. But even knowing that she had made that choice, I wanted to make sure that the child was taken care of. So, I watched her grow up from a distance."

"I can't believe you did that." He opens the photo album to see pictures of Kamryn throughout the years. From age three up until she graduated high school. Some pictures are from a distance and some are close-up. But there is no doubt all the pictures are her. "Love, how did you?"

"It doesn't matter how I did it, it only matters that I did it for you."

"Zy. This is amazing love. I don't deserve this and I don't deserve you." Eric's eyes begin to water again and tears immediately rush down his face.

"Earlier, you asked me if it was ok to invite them to the party. Are these the people you were referring to?"

"Yes. Yes, it is." He continues to flip through the photo album.

"When were you going to tell me who they were? Who they both really were?"

"I was going to have a family meeting that day once they got here."

"Do you really think that would have been appropriate? Didn't you think I would deserve to know who was being invited into my house? You wanted to openly bring the woman you had an affair with and the bastard daughter it produced into my home. The home where I raised our boys. The home that is my place of peace. The home I built for us. Did you really think that was fair to me and to our boys?"

"I didn't look at it that way. I thought telling you all at once, would be the best option."

"You're not that fuckin stupid Eric. You can't be."

"Love, I don't know what to do. I don't know if you'll ever be able to forgive me. I don't know if you're even able to accept Kamryn into this house or our lives. Yes, you've watched her grow and created this photo album of memories for me but having her here in the flesh is a different animal all together. I don't know where this is going to go or even if she will want to be a part of our lives, but I want to find out. I know this is a journey I cannot walk alone. I need you with me."

"I have one request. I want to meet Helen first. I want to sit down and talk to her before they come to our home. Do you know how to get in contact with her?"

"I have her cell phone number in my phone."

"Ok. I would like to meet Kamryn as well. But I need to talk to Helen as a woman and as a mother."

"I understand love."

"Ok, can you contact her and ask her if she's willing to meet with me face to face?"

"Of course."

"Then it's settled. We will all meet, the four of us, and afterwards we will invite them to the party. But, you must talk to Eric Jr and Maleek and let them also know they have a sister."

"I will love. I promise."

"Alright."

Eric pulls his phone out of his pocket to send Helen a text. After a few minutes, she texts him back to let him know she'll be in town in a few days as Kamryn has another meeting with that Vysin Records. She also agrees to the four of them meeting for dinner. Eric responds with a "thank you" and informs her that he will pass her phone number to Zyera, who will make the reservations. Helen does not respond. He exhales deeply and sends a group text to his sons. They arrange to speak via facetime. Michael and Maleek will come to the house and Eric Jr will call.

Chapter Eighteen

After meeting with the Vysin Records all morning, Lena asks Kamryn and Helen to lunch. Helen declines and says she has some things to take care of and tells Kamryn she'll see her later. They exchange hugs and Helen walks in the opposite direction of the two ladies.

"Is there any place in particular you would like to go for lunch Kam?" Lena asks her as they walk towards Lena's car.

"No. Where ever you choose is fine with me."

"Great. I know this great little restaurant on Sexton Street that Michael loves to take me to. I figure you might like it as much as I do. It's pretty quiet and quaint."

"Sounds good to me." They get in Lena's car and she pulls out of her parking spot.

"I can only imagine how excited you are about everything. This is a great opportunity for you." Lena says as she drives down Michigan Ave.

"I'm speechless really. It seems like so many things are happening all together. I can't believe how fortunate I've been. First my job at Horns, then being able to sing there, then finding out who my father really is, and now the possibility of becoming a true recording artist."

Lena can't believe Kam spoke so lightly of finding out who her father really is. "Do you want to talk about any of it with me?"

"Yes, it's fine. It doesn't bother me at all. Nothing happens by accident. This is fate."

"I guess not." Lena says as they continue to walk towards her parked car. "Have you spoken to Eric directly yet?"

"No. My mother told me that he and his wife want to meet us together and talk. We're going to dinner tomorrow night with them. My mother's a little nervous. Instead of going to lunch with you, she went shopping to find a new dress to wear." Kam laughs quietly. "I don't know why she's so nervous though. They're people just like us. And my mom has done an amazing job raising me."

Lena looks over at Kamryn and smiles. Every time she speaks with Kamryn, she becomes more and more impressed by her. "Yes, she has Kam. She has done a great job."

"Did you know that Michael was my brother?"

"At first, no. He told me shortly after he found out. Just so you know, he's excited to have a little sister. I know that he hasn't said anything to you about knowing. And you obviously haven't said anything to him. But I'm glad that you know and I'm even more elated that he knows."

"At first, I was pissed. Then after she told me the full story, I understood why she never said anything. Growing up with her and my grandparents, I didn't have a bad life. I was loved and cared for. I don't feel like I really missed anything. But then again, you can't miss what you've never had. Now that I know, it doesn't change how I feel about her in the least. She's still my best friend and I have a more profound love for her honestly. She could have told him but it was her decision not to."

"That's a very mature way of looking at it."

"It's the best way for me to look at it. I would like to get to know him, my father. If he's half the man that Michael is, then it would be cool to have him in my life for real. I mean, I don't harbor an ill will towards him for not being in my life this far. You can't help what you don't know and he didn't know because she chose not to tell him she was pregnant. Now that he knows, it's up to him to decide if he wants to get to know me. I won't force myself on him or make him feel guilty for the past. I'm all about moving forward. The ball is in his court. I'm open to playing. It's not like my Mama told me someone else was my father or that my father was dead. We just never spoke of him."

"I get it and to be completely honest with you, I don't know what Eric will do. But it's nice to know that you are open to letting him in."

They drive a little while longer and have small talk. Lena admits to herself that she is impressed by the maturity of Kamryn and is surprised by how she looks at life entirely. Her mother did one hell of a job raising her on her own. They walk into the restaurant and are seated immediately in a booth by the window. After a few minutes, the server appears and they place an order.

"How long have you dated Michael?"

"Almost two years off and on. It's been more in the on switch though within the last year. He won me over and now I couldn't imagine my life without him."

"Does he feel the same about you?"

"I believe so. He asked me to marry him." Lena drinks from her water glass.

"He what? What did you say?"

"I said yes. What do you think I said?"

"I was about to say you have got to be crazy if you didn't say yes. When I first met him, I swooned a little bit. He's fine. Now that I know he's my brother, I can't express how happy I am that he never showed any interest in me whatsoever. That would have been a complete mess if something would have happened." Kam laughs at own words.

"Me too. Not only have you gained three brothers but you are gaining a sister too."

"A very smart and successful sister. What do you know about my brothers?"

"They're all very successful in their own rights. You already know Michael owns Horns and the Coffee Café chains. Maleek owns and manages a few gyms, a health and nutrition company, and staff of personal trainers. Eric Jr. Is an attorney, I believe a state's attorney, in Atlanta. All three have made a very good life for themselves. They are very tight with each other and their parents are involved in their lives. If Maleek and Eric Jr are like Michael, they will be very pleased to meet you and even more excited to get to know you for themselves. As brother's go, you couldn't get a better trio than them."

"Wow. And what do you know about my father and his wife?"

"Believe or not, I've only met his father a few times and I've never met his mother. The boys are super close to their father. Michael calls him, his best friend. Right now, Michael is the only son who knows who you are. I think sharing this information has made their relationship even more special. I've noticed the change in Michael when it comes to you even though it's a new development. Once he found out you were his baby sister, he started making calls to fraternity brothers, business contacts, and friends who are in the music business. The night Gavin came to see you sing, there were at least seven other music execs at Horns. Michael trusts Gavin the most though and that is why he wanted you to sign or think about signing with him."

"Are you serious?"

"Dead ass serious. Michael does not play any games when it comes to his family."

"Wow! I can't believe he did all of that for me."

"That's who he is sweetie. That's one of the reasons I love him so much. He's an incredible businessman too. He's the reason Horns has been so successful. Most businesses don't begin to really make money until they've been open for a few years. Michael was showing a return on his investment within the first eight months. That's an amazing feat for any new business. Especially a bar or club. Those are the hardest to turn a profit. But he made it happen and after the first year and a half, he's thinking of expanding to another city."

"That's so amazingly awesome. You are very lucky to have him in your life."

"And now, so are you my dear girl." She pats Kamryn's hand and they enjoy the rest of their lunch together. Kamryn asks more questions about the brothers, trying to soak in as much information as she can about her newly found family.

"I hope to meet the rest of them soon."

"I'm sure everything will work out." Lena's phone rings. The screen shows Michael's name and Lena smiles as she picks up the phone. "Excuse me, it's Michael. Hi honey."

"Hey love. What are you doing?"

"Eating lunch with your sister." Lena says and winks at Kamryn.

"What did you say? Is she sitting right there?" Michael's voice sounds panicked. "Why would you say that? Does she know?"

"Yes baby. She knows. We were just talking about you actually."

"How is she? How did it go today?"

"She is fine. We met with the Vysin Records and talked about contracts but have not signed anything. There were some things in the contract that I didn't feel were in the best interest of Kam. I suggested some changes that would be better suited for her and her career. Financially, I didn't like the money and there is no way I was going to let them try to get over on our little sister. Not on my watch." Lena looks up at Kam who is smiling as she continues eating her lunch.

"How is she about the sister thing? Does she have any questions?"

"Wouldn't you if you just found out who your family was? She's ok though. I'm really impressed by her baby. She is surely your sister. You should spend some time with her."

"I will. Thank you love. Thank you for looking out for her."

"It's my pleasure. Are we still on for dinner later?"

"Definitely. And some dessert too." They both laugh. "I was calling because Mama wanted me to invite you to her July 4th family celebration."

"Really? That's new."

"Not really. Well, maybe a little. But Eric Jr and his family are coming in town and she wants a full family get together this year. And she told me to bring the young lady I was dating. So, young lady, you have been invited."

"Well sir, in that case. I accept the invitation."

"Good because I had already told her you were coming."

"I bet you did." She laughs again.

"Alright love. I gotta go. The distributer is here with the new stock for the bar. I'll see you later baby."

"Ok. Later." She hangs up and places her phone back into her purse. "That man of mine." She looks at Kamryn again and they both laugh.

"He sounds like a handful."

"He's your brother and your boss. I'm sure you've seen him be a

111

handful before." They share another laugh.

Chapter Twenty

Dinner reservations were made for 8pm at LaCris St. Croix, the city's most exclusive French restaurant. It's intimate table settings are ideal for those who wish to have privacy in a public restaurant. The booths have high back which absorb sound and large table so all can be comfortable. Helen and Kam arrive just as Zyera and Eric are being approached by the maître d. Eric sees Kamryn first and smiles at being face to face with her for the first time.

"Hello Kamryn." He reaches his hand out to shake hers. She looks at his hand then to her mother. The love in her mother's eyes is evident. Kamryn looks back to Eric and steps forward, allowing him to embrace her as a father should. "Oh, my goodness." He says as he holds back tears.

"Hello Daddy." She says finally and closes her eyes. She too begins to feel emotional.

"Oh, baby girl." Eric says and looks right into the eyes of Helen. She nods her head at him as if to say, 'it's ok.'

Zyera steps to the side of Eric and Kamryn and reaches her hand out to Helen. "Hello Helen. I'm Zyera. Finally, we meet in person."

"Yes, finally. Thank you for the invitation to dinner."

"Thank you, for accepting." Both ladies look at the father and daughter still embracing each other for the first time. Zyera taps Eric's shoulder. "Love, they are waitin to seat us at our table."

Eric finally releases Kamryn and the four follow the maître d to the reserved booth. At the table, Kamryn and Eric sit in the middle to sit by each other and Helen and Zyera sit on the ends.

The four sits in silence at the table with only the intermittent sounds of the inhale and exhale letting each know the other is still alive. Zyera staring at Helen and Helen staring back. Eric gazing lovingly at Kamryn and Kamryn scanning his face for features she sees in herself. Each not really knowing what to say and none wanting to say the wrong thing. Eric looks at both women, knowing that all of this is his doing and that it's up to him to start a conversation. Any kind of conversation. But what does he say that is not going to start an argument or cause someone to be uncomfortable? He looks back at Kamryn and puts his hand on hers as it sits on the table top.

"You are beautiful." He says to her with all the love he can muster without crying.

"Thank you." Kamryn smiles back at him. "I'm guessing I look more like your family than Mom's."

"Yes. You have a lot of my mother's features. My oldest son, your big brother, has the same features. Her cheekbones and her eyes. Your mother told me your eyes were the same color as mine when you were born."

"Yes. I've seen the pictures where they were. It's nice to know where they actually came from."

"Well my beautiful girl, now you know." He squeezes her hand out of love and affection. "Is this weird for you?"

"Not really. I mean, I knew I had a father even though I didn't know much about who you. Growing up, my mom didn't speak about it, so I didn't ask. I always wanted to meet you and know you and I hoped I would get to meet you one day. That day has come."

"You seem to be very comfortable with this whole thing Kamryn." Zyera says to Kamryn finally pulling her gaze away from Helen.

"My Mom taught me to take life as it comes. This is something that has come to me. I welcome it with open arms because I am a part of him. Just as I hope to one day be a part of your family." Kamryn says.

"You are surely an amazing young woman." Zyera tell Kamryn. "Helen, is it ok if we go speak privately for a few minutes?"

"Yes, of course." Helen responds and both ladies get up from the table. "We won't be too long Kam."

"I'm ok Mama." She smiles at her mother and watches her walk away with Zyera leading the way.

The restaurant has a bar area where the ladies take a seat near the far end. Zyera selected these seats to have a little privacy and because both ladies can see the booth where Eric and Kamryn are sitting from these seats. Zyera had not prepared a speech or a monologue for this moment however, she knew that she needed to speak with Helen alone. As they settle, the bartender asks if they would like a drink.

"White wine please." Zyera requests.

"I'll have the same." Helen states.

The ladies sit next to each other with the air of awkward silence between them. Neither knowing exactly how or where to start.

"Helen, I just wanted to say thank you for meeting with us tonight. I know it had to catch you off guard to be asked. But I also know that you expected to officially meet me one day. Especially with the reveal of Kamryn to Eric."

"Honestly, I had hoped to never have Kam meet Eric. It wasn't because of you or because of him. It was because of me and my decision to not only have an affair with a married man but to bore a child from that affair. I never wanted Kam to feel like she was an accident, a mistake, or unwanted. I didn't want her to look at me in a way that made her see me different. I didn't want her to be disappointed in me as a woman or as a mother. And I didn't want her to feel like a burden on anyone whether that man was her father or not. It's true that Eric and I knew what we were doing, when we were doing it. It's also true that we knew that our actions carried consequences and repercussions. But Kam was not a mistake and if those words hurt you, that's not the purpose of them. Kam was and still is my gift. Not because she came from Eric, but because she is of me."

The bartender returns with their wine glasses. "Please put this on the tab for the booth over there." Zyera points to their reserved table. She can tell Kamryn and Eric are deep in their own conversation and not worried about the two of them. She turns her attention back to Helen. "I understand what you mean. My sons are the same for me. They are my air and my grandchildren are my heart. Without them, I would've been lost years ago. We've raised our boys to be men. Good, upstanding, God fearing men. I couldn't have done that without Eric."

"Zyera. I do want to say this to you. I apologize for my part in the affair…"

"Stop right there. I don't want your apology. That's not what this side chat is about. This is about me talking and you listening. I'm not trying disrespect you. I need for you to understand where I am coming from in this entire situation."

"Ok." Helen takes a sip of her wine.

"I had a conversation with Eric the other night that led to the request of this meeting. He finally sat down and gave me his version of the time you spent together. To say it hurt me was an understatement. To say I understand why it happened is also an understatement. To be completely honest with you, I knew something had happened between the two or you years ago. I remember the first time I saw you in his classroom and the way your demeanor changed when you saw me come into the room. I didn't say anything at the time, because I am not a woman who makes a scene and I did not want to embarrass my husband or myself in front of his entire classroom. Not to mention, he could have lost his job and I couldn't allow that to happen either. At the time, he never said anything about the two of you however my gut told me otherwise." Zyera pauses to take a sip of her own wine before continuing. "Shortly after Eric finished teaching and returned home, I discovered some information which I never spoke to him about. Instead, I took it upon myself to find out who you were and what the extent of your relationship was with my husband. That's when I found out that you were pregnant. I didn't tell him nor did I reach out to you. I waited to see if you would come to him or to me. But you never did. After Kamryn was born, I waited again for you to show up on my doorstep with your baby and ask for help. But you didn't do that either. You continued with your life as if Eric didn't exist and the fact that he was Kamryn's father didn't matter. I truly don't know if I was impressed or pissed off with you about it. And because I couldn't decide on my own feelings, I watched Kamryn grow up from a distance. You didn't afford Eric the opportunity to share a life with her so, I was there in his place. Volleyball and basketball games. Concerts and graduation. I was there or someone was there for me. Taking pictures and recording for me to see later. This may seem unrealistic to you to know that I am that type of woman or that a woman like me really exists. But I am and I did what I needed to do to for Eric. You didn't get to see what type of father he was and still is to our boys. How supportive and loving and protective he is. How he will give his right arm for any one of them. You didn't give him the opportunity to be that for Kamryn. And that was your right. But it is my duty to support him in every way that I can, whether he is aware of it or not."

Helen is stunned by the revelation of Zyera's words and past actions. Rendered speechless, Helen pics her glass up and consumes her wine. "I never saw you at any of her events."

"You weren't meant to. I wasn't there to be noticed or to have you see me. I was there to support Kamryn in Eric's absence." Zyera says. "And I would do it all over again in the same way to make sure she received that support from this side of her family." The look she gives Helen only validates her words leaving no doubt that she is being completely honest with her. "I've watched Kamryn over the years and you've done an amazing job on your own. That's a compliment from one mother to another. Let me say this. When I found out about Kamryn, I wanted to come to you on some 'Hello Barbara, this is Shirley' type shit. You will never know how close I was to knocking on your front door several times. The only reason I didn't is because even from a distance, I fell in love with that young woman sitting next to my husband tonight. As a woman, I wanted a showdown with you but as a mother, I wanted to protect her and protecting her was most important to me. I'm sure that is where your head was too when you made the choices you made. I didn't invite you here tonight to fight or argue or even call you names. I came here to see you face to face and support the man that I have loved unconditionally for more than thirty years. The hurt in his face when he told me about Kamryn and how much he wanted to be in her life, broke my heart. Because he felt that I wouldn't be supportive of it. I'm here to show him that he has my full support and to show you that I plan on being a part of Kamryn's life just as much as he is. I only have one question for you. Is that going to be a problem?" Zyera motions for the bartender to bring two more glasses of wine for them.

"Kamryn is an adult now. It is her choice to have a relationship with Eric and in turn a relationship with you and her brothers. I will not stand in the way of that and I have told her, whatever decision she makes, I will support." Helen picks up her second glass of wine delivered by the bartender.

"Alright." Zyera picks up her glass as well. "Salute, to Kamryn and her success both in family and in her career." The ladies clink their glasses together and sip their wine. Without speaking another word, they both stand and walk back to the table to join Eric and Kamryn.

"They both made it back Kam. I guess I'm going to make it through this dinner after all." Eric laughs at his own joke.

"Don't push it Eric." Zyera says as she takes her seat next to him.

"Ok love." Eric says then makes a face at Kamryn.

"Are you ok Mama?" Kamryn asks Helen.

"I'm good baby." Helen answers and leans in to kiss Kamryn on her cheek. "Everything is fine."

Their server for the night approaches the table to take their food and drink orders. After she walks away, Kamryn continues her previous conversation with her mother.

"Mama, we've been invited to their July 4th family celebration. My brothers will be there and I'll get to meet my niece and nephew. Can you come?"

"Thank you both for the invitation but I won't be in town. But Kam, you definitely should go."

"Mama, where are you going?"

"I'll be on vacation sweetheart."

"Oh, so Ma, you about to be out here living your best life huh?" Kamryn says with a giggle.

"Baby girl, I've been living my best life for years. Where do you think you got it from?"

"I get it all from my Mama." Kamryn responds and they share a laugh. Eric watches them interact with each other. Their connection is apparent and, in his heart, he hopes to one day have the same type of relationship with his daughter.

"Well, we hope that you enjoy your vacation Helen. We will welcome Kamryn into our home with open arms. I'm sure she'll tell you all about it once you return." Zyera says from across the table to Helen.

"Thank you. I appreciate you both looking out for her." The ladies nod at each other in agreeance.

During the remainder of the night, the conversation began to flow effortlessly with all seeming to feel at ease. Most of the conversation centered around Kamryn. She reminisced on events he missed while Helen watches silently. The look in her daughter's eyes as she looks at her father is priceless. And Eric is instantly in fatherly love with her. Helen's heart swells as she senses the feeling of completeness from Kam. She looks across the table at Zyera who is watching her as she watches the father/daughter pair. Again, the ladies share a silent nod.

****

"Pop, where are you?" Maleek says as he walks through his parent's home.

"Where am I usually son?" Eric says.

Maleek laughs and walks into his father's office to find him sitting with Michael. "We were waiting for your slow ass dude. Where you been?"

"Probably laid up with that fine ass woman he was with at Horns a few weeks ago. I think her name is Miracle, right?" Michael asks with a laugh.

"Glad you could make it today son. There's something I want to tell you. I'm just waiting for Eric Jr to call."

"All three of us at once? This must be some big news. You're not sick or anything are you Pop?"

"No son. Nothing like that."

"Are you broke?"

"What? Get the fuck outta here. Hell no, I'm no broke." His father laughs loudly. "If I was, would you lend me some money?"

"Come on Pop. What's mine is yours, you know that."

"Well that's good to know just in case. But no son, I'm not broke either." Eric looks at Michael who is laughing under his breath.

Maleek sits across from his father and brother and smiles. "My bad Pop for being late. I was doing somethings in my gym space and lost track of time."

"How's the business going? Any new clients?"

"Jessica told me she received some calls from some of your plastic surgery clients. Have you been giving my cards out again in your office?"

"I always have cards and flyers for all businesses related to you boys. The café, the gym and nutrition centers, Horns, and I even have some of Eric Jr's business cards there. It's my job as your father to promote you all. It's not like I'm suggesting working out instead of plastic surgery, but some of my prospective clients don't need plastic surgery. They only need to change some eating habits and gain a slight workout regime. If that's the case, I nudge them in your direction."

"Well, thanks Pop. I appreciate that." Maleek says and places his hand to his heart. "What time is Jr supposed to be calling? I have a date tonight with Miracle and a brotha gotta make sure he's looking fly."

Eric checks his watch, "He said he'd call about 5:00pm, he still has fifteen minutes. Mike, what have you been up to lately?"

"Just workin Pop. Been looking at expanding Horns and opening a club in another city. Maybe Atlanta, since Jr is there. Not that I'd ask him to get involved, but I'd feel better with family in the area to oversee some things. Plus trying to buy a space there is going to take some time and he knows all the areas that are poppin in the nightlife scene. I don't want to get a spot that is too far for people to travel but too congested for people to get to either. Since Horns is doing so well now, I think it's the perfect time to consider branching out into another market."

"I like it. That's something you and Jr can talk about next week when he's here." Eric says and nods his head in agreement looking back and forth at his middle and baby boys. His pride for them and all they have accomplished is written all over his face. He can't help but smile when he looks in their faces. Silently, he prays that Jr and Maleek will be as open as Mike has been when he tells them about Kamryn. As his mind begins to find the words to use to tell them who Kamryn is and how it all happened, the video telephone rings showing Jr's number. Eric takes a deep breath and clicks the answer button. Jr's face pops up on the television screen.

"Jr, what's up son?"

"What's goin on Pop? Mike and Maleek! It's great to see everyone. The brothers three!" He laughs.

"What's goin on with you in the "A"? Still lockin people up?" Maleek says with a chuckle.

"Come on Leek. Don't start that shit man." Jr says and laughs. "But since you asked, hell yeah. That's my job dude."

"Jr, you lookin good bruh. Hittin the gym I see." Mike says and they laugh.

"Man! Come on bruh, why you comin at me like this today. I didn't call for you to start baggin on me and shit." He laughs with them. "Pop, what's goin on that you needed me to call you with these two shiftless dudes in your house. Everything must be ok if y'all got time to be shuckin and jiving."

"Alright guys, listen up. I have something serious I want to talk to the three of you about." His words make all three of his sons sit up straight as he looks at each of them. Eric takes a deep breath. "A long time ago, I did some things that I shouldn't have. I let my dick make decisions where my head should have been in full control and at the time, I never thought it would come back to me. Twenty years ago, I cheated on your mother with another woman. The results of this indiscretion led to me fathering a child with this woman. I never knew about the child because the woman never told me. When I ended the affair, I never contacted her again. I left the whole thing in the past and dedicated myself back to my marriage to your mother and raising you three. Recently, I saw the woman again. Through conversation, she told me about the child, who is now a young woman." Eric drops his head as he feels tears of shame fill his eyes. "Your mother knows and we have already discussed some things as it relates to her and me. I was very open and honest with her about wanting to get to know this young woman and accepting her into my life. In turn, your mother has also said that she wants to do the same. I'm coming to you as your father to ask for your forgiveness for stepping on your mother and to ask you to find it in your hearts to consider accepting this young woman into your lives as well. You don't have to and I won't make you. This is just me coming to you asking you to consider it." Eric looks up into the eyes of each of his sons one at a time to try and gauge their reactions. He looks at Michael first for encouragement. Michael smiles and winks one eye at his father. Next, he looks at the television into Eric Jr's eyes. Stunned and speechless, Jr's shock is evident on his face. Finally, he turns his head to Maleek and what he sees breaks his heart. Maleek is sitting in silence staring into space with tears streaming down his face. As the youngest son of Eric and Zyera, he has always been a Mama's boy through and through. His relationship with her is unquestionably the reason why he respects women the way he does.

"Maleek," Eric moves from his seat to sit next to Maleek. "Son, say something." Eric places his hand on his son's shoulder. "Please, son, say something."

"I ... I ... Pop? How?"

"This had nothing to do with your mother and it damn sure had nothing to do with you three. It was a decision I made. And I have to face those repercussions."

"Pop," Jr says to get his father's attention. "Who is this woman? Is she someone we know or someone Mom knew?"

"No son. It's no one your Mother knew or even anyone who had ever been around you boys. It was a woman I met when I was teaching."

"Did you love her Pop?" Maleek asks through silent tears.

"I won't lie to you son. I had some strong affection towards her. I can't sit here and say it was the kind of love that made me think about leaving your mother or you boys. But it was the kind of love that made me want to be with her every chance I could. I'm sorry if that hurts you to hear."

"Pop. I understand. I can't judge you for your actions. I'm sure we're not getting the full story of what was going on with you and Mama at the time. I'm not going to sit here and say that I'm ok with what happened or your actions. But it's not for me to judge you. I'm your son and I love you through whatever. If Mama is ok, then I'm ok." Michael says hoping to shake his brothers out of their who wants to be a millionaire question session. "None of us are perfect. Shit, we all mess up from time to time. Your situation with this woman is none of our damn business. Your relationships with us, as your sons, is our business. I commend you for coming to us as a man and not only apologizing for your actions but giving us your side of this story."

"Thank you, son." Eric looks over at Maleek who is still sitting in silence outside of his one question asked. Eric knew that Maleek would take it the toughest.

"Mike's right. It doesn't matter who this woman was or is, the only thing that I care about is if Mama is alright. Honestly Pop, I remember what it was like when you were teaching. I mean, yeah, it was a long time ago and everything. But I remember Mama being sad and stressed. I remember you being gone for long periods of time and then home for one or two days and then gone again. Mike and Leek, you may not remember because you were younger but I remember. Then, I remember when you came back. You were different. You didn't miss anything after that. You were at every one of my ballgames and every football game Mike had. You went to every parent teacher conference and never missed anything including the PTA bake sales at the school. Who am I to judge you? Shit, I've done some things that I'm not proud of but the shit happened. When we first got to Atlanta, I cheated on Evelyn with this young thang from my office. When she found out she kicked my ass outta the house for three months. After a lot of begging, the promise of an upgraded ring, and a new Maserati, she gave me new keys to the house because as soon as she kicked me out, she changed the locks." Jr laughs at himself. "Now, who is this young lady you are saying is our sister?"

"Her name is Kamryn."

Maleek's head pops up and he looks directly at Michael. "The singer from Horns?" He turns his head to look at his father. "Are you shitting me? How is the singer from Horns our sister?"

"Wait, what is Leek talking about?"

"I found out who Kamryn was after seeing her mother one night in Horns. It was a total coincidence that we were both there that same night. My ass was over there trying to be charming and she tells me about Kamryn. You could've knocked me over with a feather that night."

"Did you know, Mike?" Maleek asks his brother.

"Not initially when I hired her. Hell no, I had no idea who she was. But the night Pop found out, he needed someone to talk to and he told me. Straight up, he was a mess that night after he found out. He asked me not to say anything to anyone and I didn't. Not even to you two. Besides, it wasn't my place to say anything."

"That's fucked up Mike."

"Watch your mouth son. No matter what's going on, you know I don't permit you using that word in front of me."

"I'm not trying to disrespect you Pop. I just can't believe Mike didn't tell us. Or at least me. I know Jr is in Atlanta but I'm right here. You could've told me."

"Bruh, what did I just say? It wasn't for me to tell you. And I promised Pop that I wouldn't say shit. So, I didn't."

"Maleek, son. Talk to me. I'm not asking you to become her best friend. Like I said, I'm only asking you to consider letting her into your life as your little sister."

Again, silence from everyone.

"Boys, this is not something that you have to decide on today. But I will tell you that your mother and I have invited her to the July 4th celebration your mother has planned. And Kamryn has said that she will be here. What I don't want, is for you to make her feel uncomfortable or unwanted. If you don't want to deal with her, you don't have to. But you will be respectful and cordial. She will be a guest in this house and she will be treated as such."

"Pop, I'm good." Mike says. "Now that she knows who we are and that we are her family, I can let her know that it's all good with me. You two can feel whoever you want to feel and handle it your own way."

"I'm good too." Jr says from the screen. "I can't wait to meet her."

"Maleek?" Eric looks at his son again. "Talk to me son."

"Pop, I don't know what to say right now. I need to let this process."

"Fair enough. I understand. You're still coming to the party, right?"

"Yeah Pop, I'll be here." Maleek says.

"And you're bringing your lady friend too, right?"

"Yeah Pop, I'm bringing Miracle."

"And Mike, you're bringing Lena, right?"

"Hell yeah Pop. You know I'm bringing my lady. Y'all not bout to be here all loved on and I'm sitting in the corner playin with myself." he laughs.

"Good. Jr, when are you flying in?" Eric asks his son.

"We'll be there on the second."

"Y'all staying here right? You know your mama is going to want those grandchildren close to her while you're in town."

"Yeah Pop, we're staying at the house. Well at least the kids will be in the main house. Ev and I will be stayin in the guest house so we can have some privacy. Shit, I may get another baby out of this visit." Jr laughs at himself. "Alright y'all, I gotta go. Talk to y'all soon. Yo Leek, call me tomorrow man." They all say good-bye and Jr ends the call from his end.

"Alright Pop, I'm out." Maleek gets up from his seat and walks toward the door.

"Maleek. I can only imagine what's goin on in your mind right now. But I can see the hurt in your eyes. Do what you feel is right but remember that I love you and nothing or no one can change that."

"Alright Pop. I'll see you next week at the party. Mike, holla at me later." Without looking back or hugging his father, Maleek walks out of the office and then out the front door.

"He'll be alright Pop. Give him a few days. I'll talk to him later. You alright?"

"I know he will. Thanks for your support son."

"Pop, I got you. You already know that." He walks up to his father. They embrace before parting ways. "I love you Pop."

"Love you too son."

Chapter Twenty-One

"Maleek, what do you want for breakfast?" Miracle asks from downstairs.

"Can you make me a banana, strawberry, and yogurt protein shake?"

"Ugh!! I was ok until you added the protein." She laughs as she hears him come down the stairs.

"Love, you asked me what I wanted for breakfast. That's what I want for breakfast." He steps behind her and kisses her cheek.

"That is true." She laughs as she reaches into the fridge for the strawberries and yogurt.

"And make you one too. You're training session with me is this morning and I'm not letting you skip it today."

"I want blueberries in mine."

"I'll make your shake and you can make mine. That way, we've made each other breakfast." He smiles and winks at her.

"You are trying to kill me." Miracle says as she rinses the strawberries

"Now you know that shit is not true. What would I do without you?"

"Find another girl to come here and make your shakes." She places the ingredients in the blender and pushes the blend switch.

"There is no other girl for me, only you." Maleek says as he walks over to her again and places his arms around her from behind. He pulls her into him and leans his chin on the top of her head.

"You're lucky I love you. Making me drink this mess because you drink it. I'm not training for anything." She laughs and leans into him comfortingly.

"You don't have to be training to drink the shake. It's a great source of nutrients and boosts your metabolism. You need that for our workouts. I'm not takin it easy on you because you're my woman. I've let you slide for months. Even though you're not paying for your sessions, you are still a representation of my business."

"Alright. Alright. Alright." She stops the blender and pours the shake into Maleek's drink bottle. "Can you rinse this out while I finish putting my gym clothes? Unless you want me to go to the gym in my sports bra, tank top, and panties."

"I must say that is tempting however I don't think anyone would be working out if you went to the gym dresses like that." Maleek takes the blender and turns on the faucet. "Go finish getting ready, I got this."

Miracle walks away from the kitchen and up the stairs. A few minutes later, she returns fully dressed for their gym workout. Maleek is pouring her shake into her bottle. "Let's go." He says and heads towards the door.

"My Mom and Dad has invited you to their July 4th celebration at the house. My brothers are going to be there as well and apparently, so is my sister."

"Wait? What are you talking about? When did you find this information out? And what sister and where the hell did this sister come from?"

"He told my brothers and I yesterday at the house. Called us all to get together so he could tell us at once. It felt like some bullshit though. Apparently, she comes from an affair my Pop had twenty years ago. And you'll never guess who this sister is?"

"Please tell me."

"Remember the singer from Horns? The one we went to see."

"Of course. Kamryn? Nooooo! You have got to be kidding me, it's not her. Did Michael know she was your sister when he hired her?"

"He says he didn't know. Hiring her was just one of those fluke things."

"An affair? Did you or your brothers know anything about this affair?"

"No, that's something my mother would never disclose to us. She made sure that we worshipped our father as we should our whole lives. She never spoke ill of him to us."

"Does she know about this daughter now?"

"Pop said she knows and that she invited the girl to the party. I don't want to go but I know Mama would be hurt if I didn't show up. I really need your support baby. I don't know if I can do this without you."

"Baby," she puts her hand on his as he drives down the street. "of course. I got you. The real question is how are you with the news? I know how close you are with your Dad and can tell this has rocked you. What are you feeling?"

"I'm pissed the fuck off. I can't believe he did that to Mama. That's kind of why I wanna hit the gym. I need to relieve the stress of this whole thing. My whole life, my Pop has been my role model and to see that he let this happen has me looking at him differently. I used to think that nothing or no one could change how I saw him. But now, I don't know. I don't know."

"Baby. Let me say this. I understand that you are disappointed in him. I understand that you are pissed at this entire situation. But this is something that has nothing specifically to do with you or your brothers. It should not change the love you have for him. What he has been to you and your brothers is still valid and it's still who he is. Do you know what I would give to have my father here for me to just see, much less be upset with? Your father is still here. He loves you and he obviously wanted to tell you what the truth himself. It's ok to be upset. But don't let it chase you away from him. And for damn sure, don't take it out on me when we get up in this gym."

Maleek looks at Miracle as the car comes to a stop in the gym parking lot. "I know you're right. I know who my Pop is and I love him. I just don't know."

"Have you talked to your mother?"

"Not yet. I haven't had a chance to."

"Maybe you should do that before the party. Then give yourself a chance to hear how she feel and then make a decision on how you really feel."

"I love you."

"I love you too."

"Now, let's go get this workout. I have some new things I want to show you."

"New things? Damn, I knew I should not have come with you today." They both laugh at her comment.

"Alright, I'll go easy on you today." He leans in to kiss her. "You're lucky."

"We both are! That's why this works." Miracle says. They exit the car smiling and walk into the gym together. "No work for you so don't even think about going to your office. If you're going to work me out, I want you devoted to it. Today is your day off."

"Alright baby. No work, just the workout. I just hope your body is ready for what I'm about to do to it today. Come on baby, let's stretch."

****

As Lena and Michael get ready for their night out, he watches her from across the bedroom. Her beauty amazes him and her determination to be the greatest at everything she does, entices him more than any woman ever has. Capturing her heart has been a journey but it was a road worth traveling. And he knows he would do it again if he had to. Asking her to marry him was the smartest move he's made in years. The only thing left to do is pick out her engagement ring.

"What are you looking at?" she asks him. "You have the biggest damn smile on your face right now. Looking like the cat who ate the canary."

"I'm looking at my future. The woman who will give me at least one handsome son who looks like me or one beautiful daughter who looks exactly like she does. It doesn't matter to me which way it goes either. Hell, I'll take a son who looks like her and a daughter who looks like her daddy. Long as they come from you, I don't care. I can't wait to change your last name."

"I can't wait for you to change it either." Lena stops there and doesn't finish her statement. But in her mind, what she says is, "In my mind and in my heart, it's already changed. The rest is just formalities."

"Woman, what am I going to do with you for the rest of my life?"

"Love me and speaking of the rest of our lives. Have you picked out my ring yet?"

"I'm working on it love. I'm working on it."

"Don't disappoint me." she says smiling as she walks up to him. With her arms around his neck, she kisses him softly, then leans back to watch his face.

"Don't get nothin started you can't finish woman." he smiles.

"Oh, I can finish it but we have reservations that we need to get to." Lena drops her arms and walks over to the other side of the best to finish getting ready. "Now, come over here and zip me down." She says as she steps into her dress.

Michael walks up to her as she turns her back to him. He hooks the zipper clasp and pulls the zipper down to the back of her mid-thigh. "I'd like a little more leg to show tonight. I mean, if that's ok with you."

"Whatever you like baby. Whatever you like."

He steps into her from the back and palms her ass. "You don't know how close I am to cancelling these damn reservations and having you for dinner." He leans forward and kisses her ear.

"I'm hungry too. You can have me for dessert." She giggles and steps away just out of his reach. "Now, let's go. People are waiting for us."

"Whatever   you   say   love."

Chapter Twenty-Two

Today is the day that all three of my sons come face to face with my husband's illegitimate daughter. A daughter he never knew about. A daughter he didn't help raise. And in the same breath, a daughter who I watched from a distance. A daughter who in my heart, I look at as one of my own. A daughter I became invested in, just as much as I was invested in my own children. A daughter that I am so proud of in my own way. I guess life is funny that way. Maybe I'm just crazy for letting it develop the way it has. Now, though, it doesn't matter. The truth is the truth and we must face it together as a family.

"Ma, where are you?" Jr walks through the house calling for Zyera.

"I'm in the family room Jr."

"Ma," he says as he sits on the sectional next to her. "I haven't really had a chance to sit with you since we've been here. I wanted to talk to you about this whole business with Pop and this daughter he just found out about. When he told us, I will admit I was in shock. I didn't ask many questions because I didn't want to know but it's hard not to want to know. I just didn't want to pry more than I needed. Ma, I'm not going to sit here and get all in your business especially since this happened twenty years ago. I just want to know how you feel and are you ok with everything?"

"I'm not ok with everything baby but the reality is the reality and there are things you boys don't need to know about that have happened between me and you father. What you do need to know is this. I am fine. Shit happens and all we can in life is deal with it. Kamryn is not to blame for anything that has happened in the past. She is as innocent as you and your brothers are in this equation. With that in mind, I want you to give her a chance. She is beautiful, talented, and your sister. No matter how she got here or who her mother is, Eric is her father and we will treat her like family. I don't want you to worry about me. I'm ok."

"Ma, are you sure?"

"Yes baby. I'm sure."

"Ma, you are the strongest woman I know." he leans in to hug his mother and she returns the loving gesture.

"I've known stronger baby. But I thank you."

"I only speak what I know."

"Alright, now where are my grandbabies? They have to running around this big house somewhere."

"They're down by the pool with Evelyn. Jumping in and out."

"Ok. The party planner and catering crew will be here in a few hours. Just keep them out of their way."

"I'll make sure they stay out of the way Mama."

"Your father left to go get Kamryn. Michael and Maleek should be here soon with their guests. Once everyone is here, I would like for you all to meet in here to introduce yourselves to Kamryn."

"Yes ma'am." He kisses her again before getting up from the sofa.

"You boys make me proud."

"We will for the most part Ma. Maleek though is hurting more than Mike or me right now. I know it's because if his relationship with you Ma. He's your baby boy. Maybe you should talk to him before he meets Kamryn face to face."

"As soon as he gets here, tell him to come see me."

"Yes ma'am." Jr leaves his mother alone in the family room. As he walks away, she smiles.

****

"Are you ready for this?" Miracle asks Maleek as they pull up the driveway.

"I'm as ready as I'm gonna get. I still don't want to be here. But I promised my Mama I'd be here. I promised here we'd be here. I'm trying to concentrate on what she's going to think about you baby. That's my focus. You know she never likes any of the women we bring home. She never has. Says she has a sixth sense about women." He laughs as he puts the car in park.

"Well she's never met a woman like me." Miracle says with a smile.

"At least not with me she hasn't." Maleek counters. "You ready?" he turns the engine off.

"As ready as I'm going to get."

He kisses her cheek and they exit the car. Walking across to the passenger side, he takes her hand in his as they walk up the front steps and into the front door of his parents' home. In the foyer, Miracle looks around and her jaw drops open.

"I knew your parents had money but I didn't know they had this kind of money."

"Hush little girl." He laughs and gives her hand a squeeze. "Hey, where is everyone!" he yells.

"Boy, if you don't stop yelling in my house!" Zyera yells back as she descends the staircase. "Now get over here and give your mama a hug." She smiles as she reaches the bottom of the staircase and opens her arms.

"Hey Mama." He steps into her embrace. "You look beautiful."

"I always do baby boy." She says and pats his back. "Now who is this lovely young woman you've brought into my house?" Maleek steps aside and lets his mother walk past him to get a better view of Miracle.

"Mama, this is Miracle Griffins. Miracle, this is my mama, Zyera Danes."

"Miracle. What a beautiful name, for such a beautiful girl. It's nice to meet you. How did you meet my son?"

"Thank you. It's wonderful to finally meet you as well. You asked how we met. Maleek used to be my trainer."

"Your trainer. I don't get into my son's business a lot but I know the rarely takes on clients as a trainer. You must have needed a lot of work."

"Ummm, no ma'am. I didn't need a lot of work. I was just at the right place at the right time. I'm the lucky one. He's a great trainer."

"I bet he is." Zyera looks at Maleek and looks him up and down. She turns her eyes back to Miracle. "So now, you're dating. Interesting. What do you do for a living Miracle?"

"I don't work." Miracle says to Zyera.

"You don't work? If you don't work, how do you live?"

"My house is paid off and I have enough savings to take care of me for decades."

"Really. At such a young age?"

"Yes ma'am. My parents passed away when I was young and left me a significant amount of money. I'm currently looking into investing in a few businesses and possibly starting my own small business. I think what you're trying to determine is if I'm with Maleek for his money. I'm not. I don't need his money. I have more than enough. I'm educated and financially stable. I'm with Maleek because he's a good man. And I know he's a good man because of you. I know that he is good to me, because of how you raised him."

"Smart girl." She looks at Maleek again. In his eyes, she sees the affection he has for Miracle. It's a look she's never seen him have for any woman he's brought to their home. "Welcome to our home. Please make yourself comfortable." She steps forward and takes Miracle into her arms in a motherly embrace. Over Zyera's shoulder, Miracle looks at Maleek, who smiles as big as a Cheshire cat. Miracle returns the gesture. After a few moments, Zyera releases Miracle and steps back. "Go on in the kitchen and get you a snack. If you want, you can go outside to the back. I need to speak with my son for a few minutes."

"Yes ma'am." Miracle slowly walks through the first floor to find the kitchen.

"Ma, what's up? What do you think?"

"I like her baby. You picked a good one with her."

"And guess what? She's a virgin Ma. Can you believe it?"

"Shut your face! She is not." Zyera leads Maleek to walk into the family room. "How long have you been dating her?"

"Almost a year. And yes, it's been hard as hell. In so many ways." They laugh at his joke and sit on the sofa.

"I bet. I'm proud of you though. You are showing great strength and fortitude. Unless you're seeing someone on the side?"

"I'm not Pop. I wouldn't do that to Miracle. She trusts me and that means a lot to me." he says as he looks his mother in the eyes.

"Baby." Zyera looks into the eyes of her youngest son. The affection which was previously there when he was looking at Miracle, was now replaced with despair and sadness. "Your father is a good man. There were things going on back then that you didn't need to know about then and you don't need to know about now. There are pieces to this puzzle and none of them involve you. I'm going to tell you just like I told Jr, I am fine. Your father and I are fine. We are a family and that is exactly how I expect you to treat Kamryn while she's a guest in this house. Give her a chance and get to know her. She really is a beautiful girl. And," she places he palm on the side of his face, "she reminds me so much of you it's ridiculous. Almost like you two have the same mind."

"Ma. I don't want to know her."

"Evan Maleek Danes, you will not embarrass me nor will you be rude to your sister. Because that's who she is, your sister. Do you understand me?"

"Yes Mama, I understand."

"Now give me some suga and go find that young woman roaming around my house." Zyera laughs and rises from the sofa. She embraces her son again and grabs his face. "I love you, your father loves you, and we are the Danes family. Don't allow this to change your love for him. And don't use this as an excuse not to get to know Kamryn." She bends his head and kisses his forehead.

"Yes ma'am." Maleek walks out of the family room and finds Kamryn sitting at the counter in the kitchen.

"You ok love?"

"I'm fine. Are you ok?"

"I'm good."

"She set you straight huh?"

"Yeah, she did." They both laugh.

"Did she say anything about me?"

"Yeah, she asked what a girl like you was doin with a scoundrel like me?"

"Did you tell her I was slumming?"

"Something like that." He leans forward and kisses her lips. Hearing children outside, he peers out the kitchen window to see Jr, Evelyn, and the kids. "Come on, let me introduce you to my big brother and his family." They walk out the French doors and into the back yard towards the pool.

Jr sees Maleek and immediately runs toward him. They embrace and as brothers do, they start to joke on one another. Maleek introduces Miracle to Jr and they walk back towards the pool to finish the introductions.

****

Standing in the kitchen, Zyera watches two of her three boys in her backyard. This is her most favorite part of motherhood. To see her boys together has always been her greatest joy. Overcome with emotion, she doesn't hear the footsteps behind her until the arms of someone are wrapped around her midsection.

"Mama," Michael sings. "Could you be, the most beautiful girl in the world?" he squeezes her.

"Michael. It's about time you got here. I swear, you will be late to your own funeral."

"It wasn't me Ma. I was waiting on someone else." He says as Zyera turns around and hugs her son tightly.

"Well let me see who made you late." She slaps his arm, signaling him to step aside.

"Mama, let me properly introduce you to Lena."

Zyera's face freezes as she again comes face to face with Dalene McCray. "Ms. McCray. Welcome to my home. Its good to see you again."

Michael looks back and forth between his mother and his fiancée. "Mama, how do you know Lena?"

"Son, Ms. McCray was one of the Ladies of Pearl honorees this year. We met at the ceremony."

"Mrs. Danes, how nice to see you again."

"Please, call me Zyera. I didn't know you were dating my son. Michael, you never said anything about dating Dalene McCray."

"Mama, how was I supposed to know you knew who she is." Michael is still in awe of his mother's response to Lena. Never has she been impressed by any woman he's brought home to meet her and he's brought plenty.

"Zyera, you have a beautiful home. Then again, I wouldn't expect anything less. Thank you for inviting me to your family celebration." Lena smiles.

"You my dear are welcome. I must say, I never thought I'd see my son with a woman of your standing. He normally brings home-."

"Mama! That's enough." Michael interrupts her statement.

"Ok baby. I'll save that for another time." Zyera laughs and reaches out her arm to Lena. "Please, this way. Everyone is in the back waiting. We're all still waiting on my husband to get back." Zyera leads Lena through the house to the kitchen and out the French doors. The small crowd of people is reflective of the privacy of this event.

"It's beautiful." Lena exclaims.

"Thank you my dear. This is my family mostly. We are small bunch but we have a lot of love." They walk towards a circle of people standing by the gazebo. When they are close enough, Lena can see Maleek and Miracle. They are talking to another couple who she contends to be Michael's oldest brother and his wife. "Jr, Evelyn, Maleek and Miracle, let me introduce you to Michael's lady friend, Lena." They all offer their hello greetings. Maleek steps up and gives Lena a hug. Miracle follows his lead.

"Lena, it's great to see you again. Glad you could make it." Maleek says.

"Maleek, Miracle, it's good to see you too." Lena says.

"Well seems like I've been in the dark. Looks like you've met almost everyone already Lena." Zyera says and laughs. "Nice to know that you all can keep a secret. I think." Everyone laughs and continues to chat.

After socializing through the guest, Zyera looks toward the house and sees Eric standing in the kitchen with Kamryn. Zyera takes a deep breath and looks across the yard into the eyes of Michael. He apparently has been watching her. He shakes his head at her and she returns the nod.

"Please, excuse me." she says to her guests. Stepping away from the group, she motions to Michael to get his brothers and meet her in the house. In the kitchen, she overhears Eric and Kamryn laughing. "Well hello you two. What did I walk in on?"

"Hello Mrs. Danes. Daddy was telling me a joke. A corny one, but a joke none the less." Kamryn says through her laughs.

"Sweetie, please call my Zyera. You are family. And yes, your father only knows corny jokes. I think that's his only flaw. Been that way since I've met him. Now give me a hug." Zyera steps up to Kamryn and opens her arms. Without hesitation, Kamryn accepts the gesture and allows Zyera to close her arms around her. Over Kamryn's shoulder, Zyera looks into the eyes of Eric and sees his gratitude for her and love for Kamryn. It's true that a parent's love for their child is unconditional.

"Thank you, Zyera. For everything. My mom told me what you said and what you've done." Kamryn whispers as Zyera continues to hold her.

"No Sweetie, thank you for helping to make our family complete." Zyera whispers back to her.

The women step away from each other as the rest of the Danes men walk into the kitchen. Jr and Michael walk up to their father and greet him with a hug. Maleek stands by the patio doors watching his father and brothers. His eyes scan the room then stops making direct eye contact with Kamryn who is still standing in the arms of his mother. Trying to remember his mother's words from their earlier conversation, Maleek closes his eyes to hold back tears. When he opens them, all eyes are looking at him.

"Come here son." Zyera says to her youngest son. Maleek stands still, feeling paralyzed from pain and from fear. A fear he's never felt before. His hesitation to follow his mother's request is true evidence of his own agony. "Evan, please sweetheart. Come here and meet your sister." Zyera softens her voice as she reaches out her hand to her son. The hurt he feels for her can be read in his eyes. She motions her fingers to pull him forward. "Come here my love."

Slowly, his legs move as he walks towards his mother, never breaking eye contact with her as she was now his strength and guide as if he were a blind man. The small distance in which he travels to her through the kitchen feels as if he's participating in the Boston marathon. The ten-step distance feels like miles for him to reach the finish line. The kitchen remains quiet as Michael and Jr stand by their father and watch their little brother walk to their mother. The matriarch of their family. The love and guide that has been there for them their entire lives. Standing in front of his mother, Maleek searches his mother's face. The soft smile of love and support gives him courage and the light touch on his face provides the security he needs to fulfill his mother's initial request.

Face to face with the young woman he heard sing in his brother's establishment, Maleek looks into her eyes. In them he sees what he did not expect. He sees himself. He sees his grandmother. He sees his father. "Hello." He manages to verbalize.

"Hello Maleek. I've heard a lot about you." Kamryn says shyly.

Unsure of what to say now, Maleek looks at his father. The man he's idolized growing up and as an adult man. The one who taught him not only how to ride a bicycle, tie a neck-tie, and drive. The man who showed him what being a man was all about. In his father's face, he sees sadness for the anguish of betrayal his son feels. Without words, he pleads for his youngest son to forgive him for his indiscretion twenty years ago. Forgive him for the shame he has brought upon himself. Forgive him for the pain he has caused Zyera and his family. Forgive him for not knowing that this would be the outcome.

Eric walks towards Maleek slowly. The man that he is today is not the man that he was yesterday or even twenty years ago. Today, Eric Danes is the father of four beautiful children. Three boys and one girl. "Son, I'm sorry." He expresses with sincerity as he reaches Maleek's side placing himself in between him and Kamryn. "I see you son. I see your heart. You can feel however you need to feel. You can take this as slow as you want. We have all the time in the world." With no other words expressed, Maleek falls into the arms of his father. As if grasping for his own life, Eric holds on to his son. "I love you son."

"I love you too Pop. I love you too."

Kamryn views the exchange of love and support in silence along with Zyera, Jr, and Michael. The two men stand in their amorous embrace as tears cascade down the face of Zyera. Seemingly in one movement, she encloses the two in her own arms, followed by Jr and Michael, whom have come across the kitchen quietly. Kamryn feels her own emotions swell up in that moment as her own tears stream down her cheeks. Jr looks up into her face. "What are you waiting for little sister? Get in here." he states and smiles. On cue, the group opens, allowing Kamryn to step into the center. The five surround her tenderly. This is not the talk Zyera or Eric thought they would have when introducing Kamryn to Jr and Maleek however, it is the perfect introduction they could never have imagined. They stand in their encirclement for what seemed to be eternity. The sounds of children playing brings them back to the day. Separating, they look at each other.

"Hi Kamryn, I'm Maleek." He says, finally addressing her directly.

"Kamryn, I'm Jr. Michael has told me a lot about you." he steps in to hug her. "I hope you're ready to have three big brothers. We are a handful."

"I'm noticing. But I'm up for it. Michael has been like a brother to me since he hired me at Horns. Knowing the truth just makes this even sweeter. And to know I have two more like him is one of the best feelings I've ever had. I know this is unconventional, this entire experience. I just hope that you all can accept me as your sister, as I have already accepted you in my heart as my brothers." She looks at each of them.

"You already know how I feel, Kam." Michael says.

"Kamryn, you are family. You are a Danes, even without the last name officially. And you are welcomed in our home and we want you in our lives." Clearly speaking for the entire family, Zyera hugs Kamryn once more. Eric, having been quiet much of this scene beholds his children all together. It's true, it's a scene he never imagined, but he would be lying to himself and God if he said he was angry.

"Alright now, enough of all this mushy stuff. We have guests and family that Kamryn needs to meet. Let's get this party started." Zyera takes the lead and ushers everyone outside to make introductions and enjoy their time together.

Eric and Zyera take Kamryn around and introduce her first to Evelyn and Miracle. They follow up with the grandchildren and some of their closest friends. Once they knew Kamryn was coming to the cookout, the guest list changed, only inviting people who would not pass judgement on them or on Kamryn and her mother. That's not the impression they wanted to give Kamryn and its surely not the environment they wanted her to walk in to. Protecting her was as much of a priority for them now as it has been for Helen. Thinking of the career Kamryn is beginning to build, they both know a scandal such as this, can ruin her before she can get started. From a distance, they can see Kamryn becoming more comfortable with her surroundings and the people whom she now knows and sees as family.

Throughout the remainder of the day, there is one brother with Kamryn at all times. Wanting to get to know her in this short amount of time and offering her a chance to ask questions. Each sharing with her stories of them growing up. The trouble they caused together and separately. The pranks they played on each other and how it was having Eric in their corners, supporting and inspiring them to strive for the best. Making sure they don't leave out the times they were reprimanded too by their father. Giving her tips about his pet peeves and the things that he never accepted from them. However, all three knowing that since she is unquestionably Eric's last child and his only daughter, she probably already had him wrapped around her little finger.

Now that everyone has finished with the amazing food prepared by Touch of Class and dessert trays both made by SweetsByShiffawn and All You Can Sweet, it was time for the fireworks display to begin. Zyera made sure there were lawn chairs set up in the yard for those who wants to sit for the show. Zyera, Eric, Jr, Evelyn, Michael, Lena, Maleek, Miracle, and Kamryn decide to stay under the gazebo. The couples sit together, holding hands, and enjoying their time together.

"You know, I am so happy that I found you in this lifetime. I can't imagine a day of my life without you being a part of it. I love you and no matter what anyone else thinks, you were made for me. It has been said, 'A man who finds a wife, finds a good thing' and you Lena are my good thing." Michael stands up in front of Lena. Zyera and Eric look over to see what is going on. He reaches in his pocket and pulls out a black velvet box. Dropping to one knee under the dim overhead lights in the gazebo, he takes the left hand of Lena and looks into her eyes. "Dalene McCray, will you marry me?" The pause in the air creates a stillness which is imaginable with the sounds fireworks bursting in the sky.

Lena looks down at the two-carat pink diamond Michael reveals when he opens the velvet box in his hand. Her emotions cause her eyes to water and her voice disappears her making it difficult for her to speak. She nods her head as if to answer 'yes' to his proposal. Michael places the engagement ring on Lena's finger. He stands, helping Lena to her feet as they share a passionate kiss amongst the applause from all around them.

"Congratulations Michael and Lena." Maleek says as he and Jr give Michael the brotherman dap and hugs to Lena.

"Thank you bruh." Michael exclaims and Lena shows the family her engagement ring.

She reaches for Michael again and kisses him. "Now it's official." She says in his ear.

"What a beautiful surprise." Miracle states as she stands next to Maleek holding his hand.

"I know. Mike always has something going on." Maleek looks at Miracle. "That's how Danes men are I guess." Maleek reaches into his pocket and pulls out a pink velvet box and drops to his knee. Everyone starts screaming as he grabs Miracle's left hand.

"What are you doing?" she asks shockingly.

"Miracle Griffins, you are the only woman I've ever met who has been able to be all that, all that I need, and surpass what I deserve. Will you do me the honor of being my wife?" Maleek opens his box to display a two and a half carat turquoise colored diamond.

"Are you serious?"

"I can't think of a better way to spend the rest of my life than with you. Yes love, I'm serious. Will you marry me?"

The long pause of silence from Miracle shakes Maleek to his deepest core. Unsure if he should have asked her the most important question of his life in front of his family. They had not talked about marriage in all the time they've spent together, nor did he know if she wanted to get married at all. The smile that was on his face was beginning to fade as he watched Miracle for any sign of affirmation to his proposal. The silent plea for an answer is written on his face.

"Miracle, I love you with all that I am. I promise to be all that you need and give myself only to you and the life that we build. Will you marry me?"

Miracle takes a deep breath. "Yes." She answers. "Yes, Maleek, I will marry you."

As his brother had just done, Maleek slides the ring onto Miracle's ring finger. He stands and grabs her in his arms, kissing her seductively not caring who is around them.

"Well this has turned out to be one hell of a night love." Eric says to

Zyera as he stands behind her with his arms wrapped around her waist.

"I believe that is an understatement loving husband." She agrees, allowing her head to fall back into his chest. "I'm so happy we are here to witness it together as a family." She adds, looking over at Kamryn.

The shift in the direction of his wife's head causes Eric to follow her eyes and look at Kamryn. "So am I love." He pulls her deeper into his body.

****

The events of the Independence Day cookout will go down in history for the Danes family and all that attended. From the introduction of Eric Danes' daughter to her new-found family. To not one but two marriage proposals by Michael and Maleek. It is truly a celebratory day for them.

As the guests begin to leave for the night, Eric approaches Kamryn. "Well my dear daughter. What a big day you've had huh?"

"Yes. I have to admit it has been very eventful." She giggles.

"Are you ready to go home? I know it's getting a little late."

"Yes, I'm ready. I would like to say good night to Zyera though before I leave."

"Of course, sweetie. She's in the family room."

"Thank you. I'll be right back." Kamryn says to Eric before walking off to find Zyera.

Just as Eric said, Zyera is sitting in the family room with her feet up looking through photo albums. "Zyera, I'm getting ready to leave. I wanted to come say goodbye and to thank you for the wonderful time I had today. You have a beautiful family and I'm appreciative of your hospitality."

"It's not hospitality sweetie. You are family. Before you leave, have a seat." Zyera pats the cushion next to her. Kamryn sits next to Zyera. "You said earlier that your mother told you what I'd done. What exactly has she told you I've done? And if you feel that telling me will violate her trust with you, please do not disclose that information."

Kamryn turns to Zyera to look her in her eyes. "I don't think it will violate my Mom's trust in me at all. She told me that you have watched me grow up in my father's absence unbeknownst to him and to her over the years. She mentioned that you were at my graduation and some of my volleyball games. Basically, that you have been in the shadows watching me, my entire life without anyone else knowing. Finally, she said that you told her how much you had come to care for me, even when you know in your heart that you shouldn't have. I'm young but I know that says a lot about your character as a woman and as a mother. The things you've shown me today are evidence enough of how lucky your sons have been to have you as their mother and how additionally fortunate I am to be within your fold. And I thank you for that. I thank you for your silent support and your invisible appearance in my life." Kamryn leans forward to share an affectionate embrace with Zyera.

"You are welcome sweetie. You are very welcome." She says slightly rocking Kamryn back and forth. "You do know that you don't have to go home. We have plenty of room here in this big house. I would like to spend some time with you tomorrow, if that is alright with you?"

"Are you sure? After such a full day, I don't want to be any trouble."

"It's no trouble. I've already had one of the rooms made ready for you. Your mother told me what kind of clothes you like and what size you wear. Everything you could possibly need is in the room and the adjoining bathroom. But there's no pressure to stay. If you would like to go back to your apartment, I'll have your father take you there."

"Thank you. I appreciate the offer. I would like to spend some time with you. I'd like to stay."

"Good, then it's settled. Eric!"

After a few moments, Eric walks in to the family room to join them. "Yes, love?"

"Kam will be staying here tonight. I had the last room on the west wing made up for her in case she ever wants to stay over. Will you show her where it is?"

"Of course, love. My wife, the one who is always prepared and rarely ever surprised." He smiles. "Come on kiddo. Let's go have a look at your room." Eric reaches his hand out for her.

"Kam, once that's done, will you come back here. I have some pictures I would like to show you of your brothers."

"Ok Zyera." She replies before following Eric through the halls of the home.

Chapter Twenty-Three

The bathroom is full of steam and the mirror is fogged after my shower. The events of the past few weeks have been a whirlwind and just as blurred as the mirror. My mind is in a whirlwind right along with it, swirling in the hurricane of it all just as a ship caught in the eye of a tsunami. Toppling recklessly over and over with no sense of which way up. How did this all happen to me so quickly? One day I was in a place I wanted to be and the next, I was engaged. Something I didn't think would ever be a reality, at least not my reality. Now, here I am. I look at my left hand and the beautiful symbol of love from him gleams back at me flawlessly. Remembering my grandmother's words, "Never take off the ring the man who wants to marry you, puts on your finger. It is a symbol of his commitment to you and your acceptance and commitment to him. Do not break that bond." My right-hand swipes across the mirror to allow me to see my own reflection and look into my brown eyes.

"Is this what you really want? To be Mrs. Danes?" I ask myself.

"Well, what's your answer love? Do you want to be Mrs. Danes?" he asks from behind me.

Gazing into his eyes through our reflections, I see into his soul. The love and respect that he has shown me from day one has never waivered or faltered. I am amazed at the levels he has gone to ensuring that our bond is built on solid ground creating a foundation we can stand on. He walks up and stands beside me. at the sink, never breaking eye contact in the mirror. Before he speaks again, he pauses and smiles. Turning to me, he places his hand under my chin.

"I am only a man but I am a man who loves you beyond faults and fears. If you feel that this is not what you want or not what you are ready for, tell me now. If you are worried that this is rushed, tell me now. That ring on your finger does not mean we must get married this month, in six months, or this year. The ring I put on your finger is to let you know how serious I am about my love and loyalty to you, to us. If you need more time to deliberate if this is a road you want to take, tell me now. I will not be upset or angry. I will, as I always have, respect you for your decision." He searches my eyes as he had the night he asked me to marry him. "We have not crossed a line you have not wanted to cross and I will never pressure you take a step you are not prepared to take."

I look in his eyes as we stand face to face. There is no fear in his voice as he speaks to me clearly. All I can see is love.

"Maleek, you are everything I've wanted the man to love me to be. Truthfully, this is all new to me on every level. I don't feel pressured to do anything. I don't feel obligated because I'm wearing this amazing ring on my finger. I ask myself these questions because I can't believe that it's real. I can't believe that you're real. And to answer your question and my own, yes. Yes, I want to be Mrs. Evan Maleek Danes. The date and time does not matter to me. I will stand in front of a Justice of the Peace or a stadium full of people and say my vows today."

"I'm real, love. All the way real and ready to love you just how you deserve." He rubs his thumb across my chin slowly and leans forward to kiss her softly. "Now get dressed before I take advantage of the fact you're naked under that towel. And we both know, you're not ready for that. Just because we vowed to wait until our wedding night to make love, don't temp me. Eating you before I go to the office will make my day even better." he winks, slaps my ass, and walks back out of the bathroom.

I laugh and turn back to peer in the mirror again.

Chapter Twenty-Four

The lobby of Vysin Records is busy with people walking about, carrying on conversations, and prospective hopefuls playing music on their guitars. All around the room, there are men and women, young and old, listening to music through headphones, waiting to be called to give a sample of their talent. All the movies you see with scene of music companies doesn't prepare you for the real thing. My previous meetings here did not consist of me waiting in the lobby. Lena and I would walk in and immediately be shown to a conference room. However today, I'm waiting for Lena to get here.

At one time, being discovered by a producer and becoming a huge recording artist was the most important thing on my list. Then I found out about my father, my brothers, and Zyera. That discovery changed my perspective of important things as much as it has changed my life overall. Finally knowing who my father is allows me to fill the space I didn't know was vacant. His laugh, his wisdom, and his love are given earnestly and freely. I can see why my Mom fell for him twenty years ago. How I got here, doesn't matter. What matters is what I do from here on out with what I know and what I have available.

I think the most impressive thing that has come from this revelation of where I come from, is Zyera. She's not what I would have expected. I mean, she has watched me grow, welcomed me into her home, accepted me into her life, and made sure I knew that I was loved. Do you know of a woman who would do that, for a child that her husband fathered outside of their marriage? I know for sure, I don't. I guess I half expected for her to be the wicked witch of the west and block any and every opening available for me to get to know Eric and my brothers. If I was a betting woman, I would've lost that bet for sure. Spending time with her has been great for both of us. She has shared with me the times she saw me as a teen and even my high school graduation. I'm still amazed at how she did all those things.

"Kamryn." The receptionist called me to her desk.

"Yes." I say as I approach her.

"They're ready for you in conference room three. Do you remember how to get there?"

"Yes, I remember. But Lena is not here yet and we usually go back together."

"I know. I will send Lena back when she gets here. Mr. Vysin and Gavin are waiting for you now. Please join them." She buzzes the door for me to walk back into the secured area where the recording studios, executive offices, and conference rooms are located.

A little shaken, I open the door and slowly walk back towards the conference room. At the door, I pause and take a deep breath. Exhaling, I open the door and walk in. Gavin and Mr. Vysin stand to welcome me.

"Kamryn, thank you for meeting with us today. Where's Lena?" Gavin asks as he shakes my hand.

"She's on her way. Probably caught in traffic." I say.

"Yes Kamryn, we are excited to offer you this recording contract and I believe we've been able to resolve the issues your agent spoke of at the previous meeting. Our lawyers forwarded a copy of this prospective contract to your agent last week, prior to scheduling this meeting. Do you have any questions before we get started?" Mr. Vysin asks.

"Respectfully sir, I would like to wait for Lena to get here before I speak on or sign anything related to my contract with your label." I respond as I look Mr. Vysin strain in the eyes.

"It's not your standard contract, as we don't normally offer new artists the things we're offering you, including the amount of your signing bonus."

"Mr. Vysin, you have to know how grateful I am to be in this position. And I'm sure you know that being signed to a label is the dream of every person who wants to be the next superstar. But, until Lena gets here, I will not be signing anything." Kamryn states confidently.

Mr. Vysin begins to speak again, and the conference room phone buzzes. "Yes." He says.

"Mr. Vysin, Ms. Lena McCray is on her way to conference room three."

"Thank you." Mr. Vysin says and hanging up the phone. "Looks like we're about to get this party started." Gavin looks across the conference table at me and slightly nods his head as if to tell me 'good job.'

The conference room door opens and Lena walks. I exhale a sigh of relief knowing quietly.

Chapter Twenty-Five

Watching him sleep gives me so much peace. I believe in soulmates but I never thought I'd find mine. Yet, I've been blessed to do just that. Even in the beginning, it didn't feel like it was meant to be and I wasn't into giving myself nor my all to anyone. I can admit that he wore me down over these past few years with his persistence, his charm, and most importantly his honesty with who he was. I can accept you for your faults, long as you are not using them as an excuse why you are not doing something with your life. This man ... this man, is just the opposite of all of that. He is everything. Everything I want, everything I need, and everything that I deserve. My happiness is not wrapped up in him. It is amplified because of him. He stirs in his sleep and reaches over for my leg under the covers. My smile is visible and pure, just as my love for him is genuine and persisting.

His initial proposal was spur of the moment and I can admit that I thought it was just an utterance of passion because he was so deep inside me at the time, it felt like he was searching for my soul. Add to that, the time it took him to present me with a ring and most prominently meet his mother. No man asks you to marry him until you've met his mama, if she's still living. Mothers have a way of tipping the odds in her favor at times. And when that mother is a mother of strength and unadulterated love, her power is resilient. I knew of Zyera Danes long before she knew of me. Watching her face when she realized it was me who was dating her son showed that I met her expectations of what she wants for him. I'm half surprised she did not ask me why I had not told her during one of previous encounters.

Becoming Mrs. Edward Michael Danes will be a day of celebration that's for certain. Not only will we both be starting a new chapter in our lives but we'll be doing it as a family of three. Yes, three. I haven't told anyone yet, not even Michael. I'm not sure I really want to either. I don't want the stigma of a shotgun wedding because I'm pregnant. Finding out yesterday when I went to see Dr Mahoning was a surprise for me and her. I think the astonishment on her face was more expressive than my own. I place my left hand on my belly. I can't imagine it protruding out in a few months sheltering the gift that I've created with this beautiful man.

"Ok little one." I caress my stomach lightly and speak softly. "Give me some ideas on how to tell your Daddy you're here." Michael stirs again in his sleep, taking a deep breath, then exhaling and turning over on his side. The hand that was located on my thigh, reaches under my pillow as he scoots closer to me placing his forehead on up against my shoulder. "I love you Michael." He smiles in his sleep and pulls me into him forcing me to lay on my side. My body relaxes and I snuggle into him completely. The calmness of being in his arms lulls me to sleep.

"Beep beep beep." My alarm goes off and I slide out of bed. Michael continues to sleep as I get ready for my day. Finishing my shower, I hear his alarm sound for him to get himself up for the day. Part of me is happy I concluded my shower before he made it in the bathroom. He would have messed up my schedule and today I need to meet Lena at Vysin Records for the final review and signing of her contract. And that is something I know he does not want me to be late for. I love his protectiveness of Kamryn. I can only imagine how he will be with our children. Discovering he has another sibling, especially a sister, has changed him a little. But not in a bad way. It's not only apparent he wants to support her but he wants to safeguard her even more.

"Love, why did you get out of the shower already? You know I wanted to join you." Michael laughs as we walk past each other in opposite directions.

"Because what you want to do, I don't have time for." I laugh in return.

"There's always time for Jell-O."

"Not today baby. I have to get to work."

"Booo!" he pouts. "I got some work for you to handle right here." he mentions, stripping down to his bare-naked ass. "Now come get this work." he laughs.

"Later handsome." I wink at him and continue to get dressed.

"You don't know what you're missing."

"Oh, I know exactly what I'm missing. That's why I'm not coming in that bathroom. Get yourself ready for work." I laugh again.

"Don't say I didn't offer it to you and don't come looking for it later, because I'm not giving it to you." he laughs and steps in the shower.

"Yeah, right." I reply. By the time I'm completely dressed, he's almost finished himself.

"You're so slow woman, you literally started getting ready half an hour before me and I still beat you dressed."

"You can't rush perfection my love." I tell him.

"You're absolutely right. And I would never try to." He kisses my cheek and walks away. "Did you make the coffee?"

"Yes, I started the coffee maker. It should be ready by now."

"Thank you, love."

I finish my make-up and my hair. After one last check, I'm satisfied with my work and walk back into the bedroom to slip on my heels. Michael's in the kitchen making our coffee. He passes me my coffee cup, gets one last kiss, and walks to the door.

"Have a beautiful day love. I'll see you tonight. By the way, you look amazing. Give my little sister my love and tell her I said congratulations. I love you."   With   those   last   words,   he   was   out   the   door.

Chapter Twenty-Six

Saturday night at Horns and tonight it's a family affair to celebrate Kamryn's signing and her last official night singing at Horns. It's a full house to show her how proud they are. From backstage, she peeks through the curtains as Soulful Sounds plays. The bar is hopping, VIP is full, and not one table or booth on the main floor is empty. Excitement is written on her face as she closes the curtain back and looks over her shoulder at Michael.

"I can't explain how appreciative I am for everything you've done for me Michael. This is my dream and it's because of you that it has come true." She hugs her brother.

"Listen Kam. I didn't do anything. Your talent got you here. I did for you what I'm supposed to do as your friend and as your brother. All those people out there are for you and you have had this place packed for almost a year, on your talent. I am beyond proud of you."

"Yeah whatever Mike. I know I owe you more than what you want to accept. And I also know, you are one of the best big brothers I've ever had." She laughs.

"Kam, all of your brothers are you big brothers." They laugh together. "Now, it's time for you to get ready to go out there and knock those people out of their damn seats. Because Monday, you'll be in the recording studio working with Gavin and his team."

Kam jumps up and down a little with excitement. "I can't believe it! Thank you for introducing me to Lena. It's because of her my deal with Vysin is so great. She is amazing! She never backed down and she made sure I got everything I wanted and more than what I ever anticipated. The signing bonus, the records, and even the tour after the album is done. She is amazing."

"Yes, she is." His mind turns to Lena and he love for her. "Alright kiddo. You ready?"

"Yes, I'm ready."

"Alright, then let's give them a show they'll never forget. At least until you do your first tour." He kisses her forehead.

"Let's do it!" she exclaims and hugs Michael one more time then steps back.

At the curtain, he looks back at her and winks. She smiles as the walks out on stage. "Hello Horns!" she hears him say. "My name is Michael and I want to welcome you to a very special night. Tonight, we are honored and thrilled to announce our own sweet songbird Kamryn has been signed to her first official record deal with Vysin Records." The crowd cheers for her success. "Of course, the bad thing is, that means she will be leaving Horns. So tonight, is also a sad night for us because tonight is her final amateur performance on this very stage." A mixture of sad responses is heard throughout the club. "But tonight, ladies and gentlemen, tonight, she is here to bless us with her beautiful vocals one more time before she takes on the big stage. It is my pleasure to introduce to you all, Kamryn!" The crowd jumps to their feet to welcome Kamryn to the stage.

The applause is never ending and Kamryn blushes, bows, and waves as she stands on the stage. Peering up into the VIP section, she sees her family sitting together. Helen, Eric, Zyera, Maleek, and Jr all smiling with pride. She waves at them and blows kisses to her mother and mouths "I love you" to her, who sends the love right back to her. The spotlight shines on them all as Michael joins the family and takes his seat.

"Thank you all for coming tonight. This night is very special to me and I am so happy that you all decided to join me. I wanted to take a minute to that my family for coming tonight to support me. It's because of them, I'm standing

162

on this stage. And its because of you all that I'm taking my career to the next level. Thank you as well. So, give yourselves a round of applause." The room fills with whistles, cheers, and the sound of hands clapping.

"I wanted to start tonight off with a little "Sativa" by Jhene Aiko. Is that alright with y'all?"

"Yeah!" the crowd says in unison.

Kamryn looks over at Soulful Sounds and they begin playing the melody. Kamryn steps up to the microphone. Taking a deep breath, she closes her eyes, and opens her mouth, "Why you make it so complicated? Off the drink, we concentratin'. I know you won't leave me hangin'. Smokin' weed out the container. We spend cash for entertainment. There's more where that came from, that's all I'm sayin. It's me and you and we makin' arrangements. It's you and me and we makin' arrangements."

As the crowd has every night Kamryn has blessed the stage at Horns, they sway and sing along as her voice fills the air. All eyes are glued to the stage as Helen watches her once young caterpillar, blossom fully into a butterfly in front of her eyes. The smile on her face and the tears in her eyes are proof of pride in her daughter without her saying a word. She looks over at Eric, who's eyes are glued to their beautiful daughter as she places every person in the building under her spell. Zyera looks at Helen and nods her head in what has become their normal method of communication. The Danes boys watch their little sister with amazement and unchallenged love. It no longer matters that they found out about and met her less than two months ago. It only matters that she is a Danes.

The rest of the night, Kamryn feels like she is walking on clouds straight into the gates of music heaven. Every note she sings, every musical run she makes, and every song she's selected to perform is pure perfection. During her last song, she cries as she sings the final lines in the chorus. The music stops and the air is quiet. Kamryn looks across the room and smiles. "Thank you." she says and steps back from the microphone. Eric is the first to stand to his feet and cheer for his daughter's performance of gratitude and appreciation. Helen is next, followed by Zyera, her brothers, and the remaining audience members. Again, Kamryn bows to the audience then leaves the stage. What a picturesque night and it was made even more special with her mother and father here to watch her shine.

Kamryn remains backstage until the club empties. When she emerges from the back, her family is waiting for her on the main floor. Maleek sees her first and smiles a smile of pride and love. "Our superstar!" he says and claps his hands together giving her admiration for her performance tonight and the start of her career. "We are so proud of you Kam." The rest of her family join Maleek as they applaud and cheer for her.

"You were wonderful baby. You brought me to tears tonight." Helen says as she hugs her daughter tightly. "I am overwhelmed with emotions right now. You have made me so honored to call myself you Mama. Oh baby." She pulls her back in for a hug and places a kiss on her cheek. "You were beautiful up there. You look like you've been reborn tonight baby."

"Thank you, Mama. Thank you for coming tonight and always being my rock. Thank you, for supporting my dream and staying in my corner when there was only us. I know you letting me move here alone was a leap of faith on your part. I just want to thank you for trusting me Mama. That means everything to me, everything Mama." Tears begin to form in Kamryn's eyes.

"Don't you start that Kamryn. You're going to ruin your make-up and mine too."

"Yes ma'am."

"Kamryn, baby girl. I am just as proud of you as your mother is. You are amazing and being your father has become one of my greatest joys in life."

Eric stares at her in admiration. "Thank you for opening your heart and your life to me."

"Daddy, it was never a question of if I should let you in. I am a part of you and you are a part of me." Kamryn hugs her father. "And now that we've found each other, I'm not letting that slip away."

Zyera steps up to Kamryn and grabs her hands gently. "Young lady, it has been a pleasure to watch you grown and glow. I know that I'm not your mother but I love you as if you were mine. Just as your father has thanked you, I want to do the same. Thank you, beautiful girl, for allowing me to be a part of your life, officially." She laughs lightly. "Your talent is going to take you to places you've never thought about seeing. And I will enjoy watching you soar." Zyera hugs Kamryn and steps back to look at her. "Perfection." She winks at Kamryn.

"Thank you Zy. Thank you for everything." Kamryn smiles fondly.

Separately everyone gives Kamryn words of congratulations. Who could have imagined this scene? Not Kamryn that's for certain. Standing here with her mother, father, and her father's family, wife included. All here to celebrate her success in love and peace. How could her life get any better than this? In Kamryn's eyes, all her dreams are about to come true and things she never thought she wanted has come into fruition.

Chapter Twenty-Seven

Instead of going out to dinner, Lena decides to cook. Tonight, is the night that she has been planning for a few weeks. Tonight, she's going to tell Michael that he's going to be a daddy. To prepare she made a feast of steak, steamed crab legs, lobster tail, baked potato, and mixed steamed vegetables. The table is set with the plates, candles, and a small box for Michael. Everything must be perfect for this moment. Lena hears the garage door open signaling Michael arrival home, right on time. Lighting the candles on the table, she waits for Michael to enter the house. Butterflies are fluttering in her stomach with anticipation of how Michael will react and what he will say. She says a quick prayer right before the connecting door between the garage and kitchen open.

Michael walks in and stops in his tracks. "Well hello love. What do have you done?" he walks toward Lena and wraps his arms around her. "You cooked for your man?"

"I did. I thought we could do something a little different tonight. Take off your jacket and have a seat. Your food is getting cold." She helps him take his suit jacket off. He, in turn, pulls her chair out for her to sit at the table. He takes his seat as well.

Clasping hands to bless the food, Michael begins the prayer, "Lord bless this food we have received, for the nourishment of our bodies. In Your name, Amen."

"Amen." Lena says.

"What's the box for love?" he asks as he begins to cut his steak.

"It's something I for you, otherwise, it would be sitting in front of me."

"Something for me? What did I deserve to receive a gift?"

"You've done a lot. More than you think." She snickers at her own personal joke.

"More than I think? Well, am I supposed to open this now, after dessert, or in between? We are having dessert, right?" he laughs at his joke this time.

"Yes, greedy, there is dessert. And to answer your question, you can open it whenever you choose. There is no exact place or time during our meal where you must open it. Smart ass." Lena looks up from her own plate at Michael.

"Well, since there is "no exact place or time," I think the time is now." He sets down his knife and fork to pick-up the box the size of a rubix cube, tied over with a black bow. A quick shake of the box and Michael hears something inside shift. He sniffs the box. "I don't smell anything but there is something inside." He smiles. "Do I have to guess or can I just open it?"

"You can do whatever you like my love." She takes a bite of her own steak.

"No clues, huh?" he smiles slyly.

"No." she replies with a sexy smile as she continues to enjoy her dinner.

Michael sets his plate to the side, placing the box in its place. Slowly, he unties the bow and lets it fall to the side. He places his fingertips on the lid and looks up into Lena's eyes. She smizes. He continues to look into her eyes as he lifts the lid. Finally, breaking eye contact, he looks down to see what the box holds. His smile fades and in its place is a confused face. He looks back at Lena. Her face shows no signs of help as he is clearly confused by what is going on. Peering back into the box, he reaches in and pulls the two small items out. In his hand, he holds one pink soft baby shoe and one blue soft baby shoe.

"What is this about?" he asks her, continuing to look puzzled.

"What do you think? You're a very smart man. I'm sure you have some sort of idea." she replies as she eats some of the roasted vegetables from her plate.

"I mean, they look like baby shoes but it's not a true pair."

"Well, I wasn't sure what exactly to buy so I got both." She smiles and places her knife and fork on her own plate. Lena sets back in her seat and waits for his true reaction.

"What? What do you mean?" his eyes move back and forth from her face to her abdomen to the shoes still in his hand. "Lena, you're pregnant?"

Lena smiles widely.

"Lena, are you pregnant?"

"Yes." She calmly answers his question.

"YES!" Michael screams and jumps up from his seat, knocking his chair on the floor. Moving quickly, he reaches the opposite side of the table and falls to his knees. Lena places her hands on both sides of his face and leans in closer to him. "Love, you're pregnant." His eyes begin to water with excitement.

"We're pregnant, my love." She says and kisses him softly.

Michael puts his hands on her abdomen. "Oh love. I can't believe this. How did this happen?"

"I would suspect the usual way baby."

"I would suspect so as well." He laughs.

"Are you happy?"

"Am I happy? I am beyond happy. So far beyond happy, I'm in fucking space." He says.

"Good!" Lena exclaims and kisses Michael again.

"A baby? We're having a baby Lena?" he looks at her in pure wonder, seeping love from not only his eyes but his soul. "You have made me the happiest man in the world." He kisses the place where his hand rests.

"I only plan to give you the same things you give me Michael. Your love has captured my heart in a way I never thought was possible. And because of that, we have been blessed with this gift." She places her hand atop his as it rests on her midsection. "There is no other man I would want to walk through this life with. There is no other man for me. This precious life confirms that you are my soulmate at the most profound level." She stares into his eyes with trust and tenderness as she says each word.

"Love, let's not wait to get married. I want you to be my wife, tomorrow. I don't need a fancy ass wedding full of people I really don't care about. I just need you. Let's just go down to the courthouse in the morning and stand in front of the Justice of the Peace."

"What about the family?" she asks with true concern.

"This is about us. Not about them. We can tell them later. Unless you need and want a big wedding with all the bells and whistles. I will do whatever you want baby. Whatever you want is yours."

"I just want you and tomorrow, I will be Mrs. Edward Michael Danes."

Hand still on her belly, relaxing where their baby grows he looks at Lena longingly and devotedly. "Alright my love. We are getting married in the morning and by noon tomorrow you will be my lawfully wedded wife. But tonight, you are my fiancée and I am going to have my way with you." He stands and picks Lena up directly from her seated position.

"What about all this food I cooked?" she laughs holding on to his neck.

With every step he takes, he says a word, "Fuck that food. You are what I will be eating for dinner tonight." His hunger for her is written on his face.

In the bedroom, he lays her down on the bed and removes his clothes. Fully naked, he helps her to her feet and undresses her, with her panties as the final piece he removes. Michael steps back to admire her beauty, her body, and her aura. His eyes travel her body from top to bottom, head to toe. As his eyes travel back to her face, he pauses on her belly.

"Lay down." He says in a baritone voice. Lena follows his command. He steps up to the side of the bed. "Let me see." Eyes fixed on her freshly waxed peach, he licks his lips and drops to his knees. Lena places her feet up on the edge of the bed and her knees fall to the sides slowly, teasing him while delaying his full view. "Yes." The tone of his voice drops to a lower octave almost growling with hunger. Michael places his finger tips on the inside of her thighs and begins to trace circles lightly sending shivers up her spine. "Touch it." He commands and Lena follows his directions again. "Do it how you like it when I'm not here."

Using her index and baby fingers, Lena spreads the lips of her peach open, while the middle and ring fingers play with the peak of her hot box. She flicks her most sensitive spot and closes her eyes as she enjoys pleasing herself. A soft moan escapes her lips as she applies a little more pressure to gain more pleasure. Her body warms her from the core as she feels his fingers get closer to her moist center. "I want to hear you." Michael says.

"Ahhh." Lena releases the sound that is music to his ears.

"Yes, like that baby." He responds. The circles get bigger and closer to its destination. "Damn." He moans mostly to himself. "She's wet now." Michael strokes his dick slowly as he watches Lena retreat into her own imagination finding her sweet spot. He matches her rhythm bringing his nine inches to its maximum length as she come within reach of her climax. "Ohhh shit, Lena. That pussy looks so good. May I?" he asks, while keeping his distance but licking his lips.

"Ahhh," Lena is lost. Lost in her own head. Lost in her own pleasure. Lost in her ability to touch and please herself.

"Baby, please." he begs. "Baby. Don't go without me." He pleads.

Lena knows he won't move until she answers his request. She takes his hand, placing two of his fingers in her mouth, she sucks them greedily. Sliding her tongue in between them seductively, until they are as wet as she wants them. She raises her head to watch him, as he watches her lower them on her body and place them inside of her. Guiding them in and out as she plays with her clit and fucks herself all at once.

"Fuck Lena!" he strokes his dick again with his free hand. Still she says nothing. She forms her own rhythm between her hand, his hand, and her hips. Fucking herself and watching him while she does it. "Baby. This is torture. Please. Can I? May I?" he asks again now at her unmitigated mercy. There is no question about who is currently in control of this situation.

She smiles. "Yes love. Yes, you may." She finally replies to him with audible words. She moves her hand allowing Michael full access to her gift of pleasure and ecstasy. Like a man who hasn't had food in months, Michael attaches his mouth to Lena's peach and sucks vehemently. He uses his tongue as if it were a spoon, scooping all the sweet juice she releases into his mouth and down his throat. Drinking of her as if she were the last glass of water in the Mojave Desert. Lena grabs the back of his head, holding on as she knows what is about to come.

Coming up for air, Michael opens his mouth wide, extends his tongue with a small curve to the tip, and dips it in and out of her pussy. Fucking her with his tongue like it was his dick. In response, Lena matches his rhythm this time. Meeting him with each thrust to gain the full effect and feel of what he was offering her. She throws her head back into the bed in pure indulgence. Again, shivers overtake her body as he progressively speeds up. In and out, over and over, tasting the inside of her.

"Michael." She moans one hand palms his head and the other plays with her own breast. Michael looks up her body from his position and sees Lena place her nipple in her mouth and suck adding to her own bliss. Michael feels his dick get harder and start to drip.

"UGH!" he says. Grabbing her clit in his mouth, he switches the sequence and tempo of how he devours her pussy. Sucking, tongue flicking, and licking her in all the ways he enjoys, not worrying or wondering if she is enjoying him because he already knows the answer. All the sounds she releases comes from the center of her carnal nature. The most untainted and protected part of her. Unhanding himself, he wraps both arms under her legs and pulls her into him, holding her in place until he finishes what he started.

"Oh Gawd!" Lena half screams, half moans. "Please baby. I'm cumming!" As the words are released from her mouth, so are the juices Michael was waiting for. Like sweet nectar from the rarest fruits in the world, she quenches his initial thirst for her. Her body shakes with convulsions as Michael continues to lick and suck the tender place that just exploded in his mouth. Soft kisses are placed on her throbbing peak, to allow her time for her body to calm before he gives her this nine-inch pipe he has waiting for her. Gently rubbing his hand up and down her thigh, as her breathing returns to normal.

Michael stands to his feet with his dick at attention, pointing right at its intended mark. He continues to stroke himself while she watches. Lena smiles slyly. Shifting her body to be fully stretched across the bed, she motions for him to come to her. Michal climbs onto the bed and straddles Lena's body. In one swift movement, she lowers herself, positioning her head to receive his beautiful chocolate pipe from above. He smiles and leans forward, placing the tip of his dick in her mouth, and his hands flat on the bed above her head. She grabs his hips as he begins to pump slowly in and out of her mouth. Her lips close around his cocoa shaft as she takes every inch of him in her mouth. She moans from pure delight as keeps her eyes closed to savor each second.

She raises her forearm to halt him pump in mid-air to suck the head of his dick like a tootsie pop. "Lena. UGH!" Michael groans deeply. "Shit!" She smiles to herself and applies a little suction to her actions. "AHH!" he moans. "YES!" she removes her forearm signaling him to begin pumping. Contracting her throat, she squeezes. "SHIT!" he exclaims. "What the fuck Lena!" Shifting his weight to the left, he places his right at her throat. Again, Lena smiles up at him while he peers down at her with obvious gratification written across his face. He returns the smile and pumps faster as he tries to activate her gag reflex. Lena relaxes her throat so give him full access to what he is looking for.

"Yeah...just like that." He says squeezing her throat just a little. "Just like that." They maintain eye contact, neither daring to blink. "You tryin to me cum?" he smirks and slows his pace until he pulls wholly out of her mouth. Michael lowers his body to match hers, using his knee to push her legs apart. His hand trails down the curves of her body, resting on her hip. "You are too much." He smiles and kisses Lena, sucking on her bottom lip.

"Look who's talkin." Lena responds.

The hand once resting on her hip, moves down to the back of her knee. He raises her leg and plunges deep inside her, taking her breath away. The light in Lena's eyes turns to fire as round three begins of their love making. Rotating her hips, she meets his strokes with every thrust. Moans of pleasure and bliss envelope the room as she feels his dick swell inside her, massaging her walls. Lena closes her eyes as Michael takes her body to a height he's never taken her before. She feels her climax approaching and grasps hold of his shoulders as if she were drowning and he was the only life jacket.

"Michael." she whimpers as her orgasm flows from her body seamlessly. The warmth, wetness, and pulsating vibration of her walls causes Michael to reach his orgasm with her.

"Ahhhh!" Michael moans from the release of his own orgasm. He shakes slightly but doesn't collapse onto Lena's body. After pulling himself out of her warm peach, he goes into the bathroom to start the shower. Lena follows and they step into the steaming glassed shower stall to clean themselves before getting into bed.

He washes her completely, then himself. Stepping out of the shower first, he wraps a towel around his waist before reaching for her towel to wrap around her body. Pulling another towel from the shelf, he dries her exposed skin, leads her back into the bedroom, and puts her to bed.

"I'm going to clean up downstairs. Go to sleep. I want you well rested for tomorrow. I'll be back up when I'm done. Do you need anything?"

Looking exhausted, Lena gazes at Michael, "No baby. I don't need anything except you." she reaches up to touch his face.

"You have my baby. I'll be back up soon." He kisses her forehead and tucks her in bed.

Before drifting off to sleep, her mind thinks back on their journey together. "Thank you for a man I can build with, save with, grown with, and stay with."

Chapter Twenty-Eight

A knock on the door quiets the room.

"Come in."

"It's time sweetheart. Are you ready?"

She looks around the room at all the eyes of love looking back at her affectionately. After a deep breath, she responds, "I'm ready." And smiles.

"Then let's get this party started." Eric says and closes the door behind him.

The ladies in room give her one last hug before leaving her and Zyera in the room alone for last looks and primps.

"Are you really ready Miracle?"

She looks at Zyera with shy eyes. "Can I be honest?"

"Of course, dear girl." Zyera sits on the bed.

"I'm scared to death. My knees are knocking together under this dress. I don't know if I'm more worried about the ceremony or the honeymoon. I've waited to be intimate with anyone for my own reasons and now that it will happen in less than 24 hours, I'm petrified. Is that normal?"

"Oh, my dear girl. What you are feeling is absolutely, normal. Especially because you've waited so long. My son is a lucky man. He's a good man. And he knows that he doesn't take care of you, he's going to have to answer to me, because I've already claimed you as my daughter." She smiles. "If your mother was here, I'm certain she would be so proud of you at this very moment. Just as I am proud of you."

"Thank you Zyera." Miracle smiles as a tear drops from eye.

"Alright honey. Don't mess up your make-up. And from this day forward, you can call me Mama. If you want to."

"I would love to. Thank you, Mama."

"No tears. I can't have you walking down that aisle with tear stains. Evan is going to think I hurt your feelings on your wedding day." Zyera hugs Miracle one last time. "Alright, look in the mirror." She turns Miracle around to look in the full-length mirror. "This is the last time you will look at yourself as Ms. Miracle Griffin. The next time you look at your reflection, you will be Mrs. Evan Maleek Danes."

Miracle smiles at herself. Her eyes shift to Zyera's and the share a quiet moment.

"Alright dear heart. Let's go. My son is waiting for his beautiful bride." Miracle leads the way down the stairs as Zyera helps with her dress from behind. Her bridal party waited for her by the French doors leading to the large stone patio. The wedding planner stands at the door, giving direction and lining the ladies up.

"Ok ladies. Let's show these people how it's done."

The music begins as the guests anxiously await the dissention of the bridal party down the aisle. The four bridesmaids, matron of honor, and the flower girl meet at the alter and stand together facing the groomsmen and the groom. The music changes and Kamryn steps up to the microphone placed on a stage, positioned on the left side of the gazebo. The curtained trellis at the bottom of the stoned patio staircase shields the bride from view. As the curtain is pulled back by the ushers, Kamryn begins to sing and the guests rise to their feet to welcome Miracle as she walks down the aisle toward Maleek.

"I am ready for love, why are you hiding from me." Miracle begins her march toward her future while Kamryn sings her rendition of the India.Arie song exquisitely. "I quickly get my freedom, to be held in your captivity. I am ready for love, all of the joy and the pain. And all of the time, that it takes. Just to stay in your good grace. Lately I've been thinking maybe you're not ready for. Maybe you think I need to learn maturity. They say watch what you ask for, cause you might receive. But if you ask me tomorrow, I'll say the same thing. I am ready for love. Would you please lend me your ear? I promise I won't complain. I just need you to acknowledge I am here. if you give me half a chance, I'll prove this to you. I will be patience, kind, faithful, and true. To a man who loves music. A man who loves art. Respects the spirit world and thinks with his heart. I am … I am ready for love. If you'll take me in your hands. I will learn what you teach and do the best that I can. I am ready for love. Here with an offering of my voice, my eyes, my soul, my mind. Tell me what is love to prove I am ready for love." With the last note, Miracle reaches the alter and stands in front of Maleek.

The tears in his eyes say more than any words which will be spoken today. Miracle feels the love immersing from his soul as he stands in front of her in awe of not just her physical beauty but her spiritual purity. "You are everything." He whispers to her.

Pastor Richards steps up to the couple. "Please be seated." The guests retake their seats. Maleek and Miracle grasp hands at the alter and face the pastor. "Dearly beloved…" Pastor Richards goes through the ceremony reciting the words he's prepared to marry Miracle and Maleek. Throughout his speech of short scripture, the couple look at each other intermittently. "It is time to join the sands of Miracle and Evan. Two separate people will now make one." The matron of honor and the best man hand the bride and groom their sand glasses. Pastor Richards holds the unity pitcher. Together, they pour their sands into the unity pitcher in the shape of the infinity symbol. "The combining of the sand signifies the joining of their spirits as one in this new life." Pastor Richards sets the unity pitcher to on the table in the center of the gazebo. "The rings please." The rings are blessed by the pastor and the vows are repeated by Miracle and Maleek. "I now pronounce you Husband and Wife. You may salute your bride." Maleek kisses Miracle with a combination of love, trust, faithfulness, passion, and lust. Everyone stands to salute the couple as they turn to jump the broom and walk down the aisle for the first time as Mr. and Mrs. Evan Maleek Danes.

Throughout the reception, they thank their guest, dance, laugh, and follow all the traditions of a wedding reception. From the garter belt to the throwing of the bouquet. They eat, drink, and enjoy the day into the evening. Their family and friends enjoy themselves and celebrate today's event with love in their hearts and little cares on their minds. Miracle can't remember the last time she smiled so hard and so much. This day with Maleek by her side has been heaven and perfection. A day she will remember for the rest of her life. Her fairytale come true with her own Prince Charming. At 7:30pm, the couple walks out of their reception and into the awaiting limo scheduled to take them to the airport for their week-long honeymoon in Bora Bora.

Sitting in first class, they hold hands and stare into each other's eyes. "We're married." Miracle says to Maleek.

"I know, love." He says and kisses the back of her hand. He leans closer to her to whisper in her ear, "I can't wait to get you naked. My dick is hard right now, just thinking about it." he takes her hand and places it on his dick. "I'm going to eat you up, literally." He growls deeply and she giggles.

The pilot's voice comes over the intercom with his welcome speech and flight information. The flight attendant stops by us and asks if we need anything. Maleek orders two glasses of champagne and strawberries. She returns three minutes later with the order and advices us the plane will be taking off in five minutes. After she walks away, we toast to each other and our love. As instructed, the plane taxis to the runway and takes off smoothly.

Miracle decides to take a nap on the flight. As she sleeps, Maleek gazes at her and realizes how blessed he is to have found her unexpectedly. The favor shown to him is beyond explanation and at that moment, he makes a silent promise to God, to be all that Miracle needs him to be. He promises to be her shield and her strength. To lead how he has been taught and to always keep this moment in his heart. Ending his prayer, he says, "Amen."

Chapter Twenty-Nine

Sitting in the sunroom, memories of the past year play through Zyera's mind. From meeting Helen and Kamryn to Michael and Maleek getting married, it has been eventful and surprising. Looking back, there is not one thing that she would change. The things she experienced and watched her children experience has increased her respect for the women whom have entered her life and joined her family. She learned things about herself as well which is helping shape her into a better wife, mother, friend, and sister.

I was a little upset that Michael and Lena decided to go to the Justice of the Peace. They were married without the presence of Eric or me being there. However, when they came to see us afterwards, to let us know Lena was pregnant, I instantly forgave them. Now, instead of having another wedding, I'm planning her beautiful baby shower. That's a fair trade-off in my book. Lena fits Michael perfectly. Her drive will encourage him to achieve all the new ventures he's dreaming of and her focus will keep him on track with his future goals.

Watching my baby boy marry Miracle, was one of the most breathtaking moments of my life. I couldn't have picked a better woman for Maleek. Her pure heart and innocence has tamed him in a way I never thought was possible. Watching him, watch her, as she walked down the aisle towards him that day erased any concern I had and validated what my heart was seeing in them both. He had the same look Eric had watching me on our wedding day. His eyes popped and I could feel his heart racing from where I was standing. And I was beyond proud.

"What are you doing love?" Eric brings her a mimosa and sits next to her.

"Just thinking about the year we've had." She sips her mimosa and looks at her husband. "I wasn't sure if we were going to make it through honestly. At least, I didn't know if we would make it out together. The full revelation of Kamryn not only to each other but to our boys was something I thought would break our family. And then all at once, Michael and Maleek were engaged, married, and Michael and Lena are giving us our third grandbaby. It has been one hell of a year."

"Love, I can't apologize enough for the past and to have you still sitting here, next to me, as my wife, it means more than anything in the world. You are and have always been my rock. You have shown me more about who you are in this past year than I ever expected after 30 years of marriage." His eyes begin to water. "The love and acceptance you have shown for Kamryn, is something I can never repay you for, something I can never thank you enough for. How you watched over her then and are watching over her now, is unexplainable and damn near impossible to comprehend. If I hadn't watched you do it, I wouldn't think it was possible. Baby, I love you. I have been in love with you for over 30 years and I will continue to love you after they put me in the ground. If you would've decided to leave me, I would've given you everything and walked away with the clothes on my back but I would've come back every day begging for you to take me back."

"Eric, you are my husband. For better, for worse, for richer, and for poorer. Those vows mean something. Watching our boys commit their lives to women of worth, reminded me that we raised them with the values that we hold dear. The vows we promised to each other didn't just cover the days of rainbows and sunshine, it covers the days of thunderstorms and hurricanes. I guess that's why I never left, even after finding about Kamryn years ago. Don't thank me for staying or continuing to love you, that's what marriage is about. Coming through the storms as they approach, together."

"Watching Maleek take this next step in his life has made me so proud. All three of them have surpassed my expectations for them. They have found good women who will hold them accountable for their actions and push them to be the greatest men they can be. That is all I can ask for." Eric says looking out the window into the backyard.

"Not only have we gained Kamryn, but we've gained two more daughters. Our family is growing baby. The world continues to turn and we continue to move forward. And we will move forward as the team we have always been." Zyera turns to Eric. "We are the Danes." She kisses him passionately. "Now, take me upstairs and show me how much you've missed me." she winks.

Eric stands putting his hand out for Zyera to grasp. With a smile, she takes his hand as he helps her to her feet. After kissing her cheek gently, he leads the way through their home, up the staircase, and to their bedroom. Zyera crosses the threshold and closes the door behind them.

About the Author

Tanisha N. Bowman is a mother, Veteran, and author. Born and raised in Youngstown, Ohio, she is the daughter of Beatrice P Bowman and John E Burroughs. After graduating from Woodrow Wilson High School in 1994, she entered the US Army and served from 1994-2002. Her military awards include two Army Commendation Medals, two Army Achievement Medals, two Good Conduct Medals, National Defense Service Medal, Armed Forces Expeditionary Medal, and Army Service Ribbon. Following her military service, she attended Trumbull Business College where she obtained degree in Social Science.

Tanisha's published novels include Breeze Bye and Breeze Back, published by LFF Publishing and The Transitional Woman also published by her self-publishing company Soldier Gyrl Publications.

Thank you for your support!

Please leave a review on Amazon or on our Facebook page:

Soldier Gyrl Publications